CW01081176

TRUST ME

CATE BELLEROSE

Copyright © 2018 by Cate Bellerose

All rights reserved.

No part of this book may be reproduced in any form or by any
electronic or mechanical means, including information storage
and retrieval systems, without written permission from the
author, except for the use of brief quotations in a book review.

This is a work of fiction. Any similarities to real people, places,
or events are entirely coincidental.

Trust Me: A BDSM Romance

April 10th, 2018

SIGN UP FOR MY NEWSLETTER

Get updates on new stories, ARC invitations and other news right in your inbox!

Sign up for Cate's Steamy Newsletter at
http://catebellerose.com/newsletter

TRUST ME

1

MIRANDA

"You can't just stand around forever, Miranda. Get out there. Play a little. It's just whips and chains."

She's right, mostly. About the whips and chains at least. As for standing around forever, I think I can definitely do just that. Pressed up against the wall in a BDSM club on Flogger Friday, we're well out of the way of the kinky activities going on around us. That doesn't mean we're not watching intently. Amber's virtually salivating at the thought of some good rope ties and a well-oiled leather flogger caressing her round ass, but as her husband Eric isn't here yet, she's stuck on the sidelines.

With me.

I give Amber an exasperated stare. "It's not the right time."

She's not really listening, her attention fixed on a couple in the play area that's spread out in front of us, her trapped naked in a set of stocks, him wielding a flogger so expertly it's like it's an extension of his arm. Pink trails light up her pale skin each time he swings, each impact eliciting a deep moan from her throat. I'm sure they're way more fascinating to watch than I am to listen to. I can't really say that I blame her.

And then Amber proves me wrong, by huffing and rolling her eyes. "It's never the right time. When are you going to realize that actually getting in there and experiencing the real thing is a bajillion times better than watching it happen? You're just teasing yourself, over and over, and I don't think you're into that. At least not like this."

She's right, of course. Well, in some ways, but while she gets that this is what I want, she doesn't get me. She doesn't get why I don't jump in, and I don't think she ever will. She doesn't think that way.

With a grin like a cat cornering a mouse, she grabs my wrist. "One of these days, I'm just going to drag you over to one of the house Doms and tell them to do what they want with you. You'll be furious at me, but you'll love it."

Her grip's not so tight that I can't easily pull away from her. She's not serious. This time.

"Maybe. Some day. But you know no one does anything here without enthusiastic consent, so your plan wouldn't work anyway."

She sticks her tongue out at me.

"What's going on here?" Come to rescue me from his wife, Eric steps out of the crowd, still in his motorcycle leathers. His face is stern, but his bright green eyes sparkle with amusement. "Did I just see you stick your tongue out, Amber?"

Her eyes widen and she holds her hands up in denial. "No, of course not. I was just—"

She doesn't get any further before he pins her up against the wall and presses his lips against hers. She mumbles something into his mouth, but it's lost in their kiss. I roll my eyes before looking away. For some reason, I can watch kinksters get their freak on in all sorts of weird and exciting ways, but when it's one of the few friends I have getting kissed by her husband, suddenly everything gets awkward.

That's me—more issues than a complete collection of Playboy magazine.

They must've finally come up for air, since Eric rumbles, "You didn't think I'd miss out on Flogger Friday, did you?"

"You wouldn't dare," Amber replies huskily.

It's a good thing he gets off on her being bratty, and she gets off on him punishing her for it, because it's about to go down. Not my first time at this rodeo.

"I'll leave you guys to it," I comment over my shoulder, making a pretense of exploring the club by myself, mostly so I don't have to stand and watch Amber and Eric being happy next to me.

"Hey, wait," he exclaims. "I didn't mean to steal her away. I can wait. For a while at least."

"You say that like I can," Amber jumps in, a decidedly bratty and teasing note in her voice.

"Knock yourselves out, guys. I feel like taking a walk, anyway." By the time I'm a few feet away, they're already back to swapping spit.

I need to stop torturing myself this way. Either just make the stupid decision and jump in, or get away from here, away from temptation, shame and guilt.

I pass a petite blonde wielding neon pink and green floggers in each hand. She's raining down blows on the back of a seriously curvy brunette who's tied to a chair. The sight of it raises excited goosebumps on my arms, but there's that voice in the back of my head—always that voice—that tells me this is all wrong.

I shouldn't like this.

No one should, and I should know that better than most. So why can't I keep away from it? My upbringing left its marks, and while they might've been made with love, they're still there and impossible to erase.

Weaving my way past enthusiastic kinksters towards the back of the room, I'm reminded by how much I want to be a part of this, and at the same time, how alien I feel in crowd of people who've managed to come to terms with what they love.

Squeezing by two leather-clad gentlemen watching the stage show, I arrive at the notice board in the back. The space is set off for anyone to use, a mix of classified ads and notices of upcoming happenings. I always enjoy reading them, even though I know I'll never respond to any. Then I feel guilty about it after.

I'm a mess. So I read the board.

MWC SEEKING *adventurous Bi M latex slut for noncommittal fun times.*

SBW SWITCH SEEKING *SBM for bondage play*

FRIDAY, April 20th, our very own Paul Cannon hosts an advanced bondage safety talk. Free admission.

. . .

SWM SEEKING *SM for edge play and bloodsports. MUST be experienced and communicative!*

Is he not flogging you hard enough? Is her discipline not strict enough? Tired of your hangups? Anxiety, depression or fear holding you back? I can help you hit your stride, or your significant other. Keegan York, kink-positive lifestyle coach. Special rates if you mention where you saw the ad.

THAT LAST ONE jumps out at me immediately. Anxiety, depression and fear holding me back? I fight back the urge to raise my hand right there in acknowledgment. Below the ad text, written in thick marker, reads, "Highly recommended. - Gabriel Carson, owner."

And then, all the way down at the bottom of the sheet is a plastic baggie stapled to it, filled with a small stack of business cards.

I don't know, though. It sounds like therapy. I tried that before, and that's not an experience I'd care to repeat. No one judges in my office, the therapist said, and it took her exactly one session to prove how wrong that was.

Then again, this guy must get it if he's got his flyer up in a BDSM club. Unless he's like that counselor Mom brought in once to "chat" with me after the time she found the leather corset in my closet, and was there to "fix me." Fat lot of good that did.

But if he was, the owner of the club wouldn't recommend him, would he? Unless this Keegan York guy scribbled that on himself. Who knows these days?

I sigh. Second guessing much? I've got his business card. That's enough info to do a little online sleuthing first to see how legit he seems. A card is more professional than a cut strip at the bottom with just a phone number at least.

Pulling my phone out of my purse, I tap in the website address from the card. Looks like it's a center with several coaches and—I knew it— psychotherapists sharing an office space. It doesn't take long to find Keegan's name among them.

Wow.

There are a bunch of qualifications and degrees on his profile, but I don't read any of them because the face that watches me from the screen is way too distracting. This guy could make a killing as a model instead of trying to attract customers with flyers. Dark green eyes draw me in, large and intense, topped by thick eyebrows. His torso is at an angle, but his head is turned right into the camera, so it's like that emerald gaze is pointed right at me. He's got short black hair with a wild curl over his forehead that makes me think of Superman. High cheekbones and a five o'clock shadow dust his strong jaw, framing a gorgeous smile, full lipped and white. He looks ridiculously kissable, in a way that makes me put my fingertips right on the screen as if I could touch him through it.

Instead, I two-finger zoom without meaning to. Jeez, get a grip, Miranda.

I'm not sure I could go to this guy for coaching or therapy or whatever it is, even if I wanted to, just because of how gorgeous he is. I wouldn't be able to concentrate. Maybe it's a sign of how lonely I've been lately if all it takes is a sexy picture to get me going, but really, that man is something else. He hardly looks thirty, but I bet he's happily married to a perfect beautiful wife, with a kid and another on the way.

And there I go again. Whatever his life is like, I doubt he'd give me a second glance. Not that that is even a thing, because all I've seen is his picture, and he's never seen me at all. I could call him, though. For help, I mean. Therapy? I shudder at the thought, but if he turns out to be a dud, at least I'd have something gorgeous to look at until I could get out of there.

Forcing myself to glance away from his portrait, I go over his credentials. Ph.D. in psychology, internships, work history. Very sterile and factual, but it doesn't tell me much about him. No kinkiness meter, but maybe that's not exactly the first thing one advertises. Unless you're hanging your flyer in a BDSM club.

I slip the card into my purse as Amber comes rushing by, grabbing my arm and dragging me towards a whipping show she claims I've just got to see. Admittedly, she's right, and the guy doing the whipping definitely knows what he's doing. He's turning his partner into a crisscross of clear red stripes with a long flogger, making her squirm and moan in her stocks. It's beautiful and sexy, but

I can't get a certain kink-positive lifestyle coach out of my head.

I need help. I know that. Much as I'd love to think I can go it on my own, I know that's not the case. God, I've been stuck in the same situation for how long now? All my life? But at least a year here at the club, where I can't keep away, yet can't bring myself to become a part of it. Even Amber, who took pity on me and basically adopted me, has noticed that it's driving me crazy, and there's no doubt what she thinks I should do, to put it mildly.

Later, when I close my front door behind me and drop into the couch in my little apartment, I pull out my phone again. I meant to check Instagram, but when I unlock it, I'm still on the web page with sexy-as-hell Keegan York staring out at me, daring me to call.

Maybe it's his gaze drawing me in, or maybe I'm finally ready to try moving forward, but for the first time in a long time, I come to a decision.

I'm going to do it.

It's almost ten, too late to call, but I'll send an email. Now, before I chicken out. I tap out a few inquiring words—okay, a bunch of them, and they're a total mess, but if I stop to fix them now I'll never send them, so one last breath, and then I tap the send button.

The email is away, and I've committed.

Crap. What have I done?

2

KEEGAN

"I'm taking off for the day, Dr. York."

Kent peeks in through my open office door, already dressed to go. There are days I envy our office manager. He's an utter madman in his efficiency with phones, messages, scheduling and all around generally making sure both me and the other therapists can focus on what we're actually here to do—help people.

I couldn't do that in a million years with the skill that he does, but he's got one thing that I don't. When the day is over, he gets to go home. He doesn't have to think about his job for about sixteen hours and can spend that time however he wants.

Unlike me, who's going to be stuck here until God knows when, going through notes, catching up on emails, figuring out how to help tomorrow's clients, how to drive in new ones and all that other shit that gets stuck in between.

Still, I can't complain. I've got it pretty good. Business is good, money is good and it's all trending upwards. I'm driving a Beamer and my place is paid up. Not too bad for thirty-two, I think.

I wave at Kent. "Have a good night, man. I'll see you in the morning."

"Sure. Don't work too late. And someone ought to ring the doorbell around eight with sushi for you."

I laugh. "I'm obviously getting predictable. You take better care of me than my own mother. Thanks."

"No problem." He waves. "Have a good one."

"Yeah, you too."

As the door slams shut behind him, I get myself a coffee. I'm going to need it tonight. A couple of presses on my fancy new machine and my cup is filling up with a hot, freshly brewed double espresso. Fuck, that smells good.

While it works, I look out the window, mentally preparing for another long evening. Spring is here. Leaves are sprouting on the large oak outside. Somehow it has escaped getting cut down to make room for another building, left behind as a little fleck of green in an otherwise gray office complex. It was a stroke of luck that it turned out to be just outside my office.

Six hours later, words are dancing in front of my eyes and I find myself spending more time staring into space than getting anything productive done. The empty sushi box is sticking out of my trash can, and I've had as much coffee as I can stomach for one evening. Time to pack up and head home.

My empty home.

One of these days I should try working less and get out a little bit. Patients aren't exactly the best way to meet people, at least not in that way. Maybe someday. I'm still young, and there's a lot of work to do. I can deal with the lonely evenings until then.

One last check of my emails before I go. All spam or irrelevant. Wait, except that one. Need help, the subject says. Probably clickbait, but it's late and you never know. You never want to leave a new client waiting too long.

I quickly scan the contents.

Hi.

Umm, I guess I don't know exactly what to write. I saw your flyer down at the club, and I guess I could use a bit of coaching right now. You wrote that you can help with anxiety and stuff like that, and I've got that in spades, so maybe this is the right thing to do? How much do you want by email? Or do I wait until I'm there? I mean, I've done therapy once before, but it didn't really go all that well, and I'm just hoping that it was a bad experience, because you sound like you might get more of what I'm going through, and I'm rambling, aren't I? I should rewrite this, but I'm a wreck just writing at all, so I'm going to leave this and click send and you can pretend what I said was meaningful. Thank you and sorry.

Do you have any available time slots?

Thank you,

Miranda Larson

Wow. That's some email. When Gabe suggested that I post up at the club, he figured it'd be a good resource for the club to have, and I think he was right. It has generated some good business, and given my personal interests, I have a better angle of approach to BDSM-related challenges than most therapists. But in addition to good business, it's also generated some weird emails.

I shrug and reread it. Not much info, anxiety at least, obviously. I can handle that.

Miranda, huh? Wonder what she's like. A sweet submissive, maybe? A conflicted dominatrix? Maybe she's cute. Not that it fucking matters. Mixing business with pleasure is trouble, no matter how you twist it. Maybe I really do need to get out more in the evenings. Something to file away for this weekend.

Anyway, I can at least get back to her before I head home. Tapping out a few words after looking up my schedule, I give her some options and let her know I'd be happy to help. A quick click on send, and off it goes.

I'm just packing together the papers and preparing to head home when my computer dings. She replied. That was quick.

I'd love the 2 o'clock tomorrow, if that's still open. Better jump in while I still have the guts, right? I really appreciate you taking the time, and the discount rate, and... yeah. Thank you!

Miranda

I'm laughing. I'm not sure why. I bet her issues are serious, and I'm sure as hell going to treat them as such, but her messages are so manic. I picture a squirrel hopped up on caffeine typing at the other end.

So obviously, I want to keep the exchange going. And now that she's piqued my interest, I'm definitely curious about what she looks like. My fingers chase letters around the keyboard as I type.

Hi Miranda,

Absolutely no problem, and please, no need to be anxious. New clients are always welcome, and we'll do everything at your pace, whatever that may be. My office is a judgment free zone, I promise. Anything you say or do here will be held in the strictest confidence. I do my best to make this a safe space where we can explore whatever concerns you, and hopefully find ways to make it better. I look forward to seeing you tomorrow.

Regards,

Keegan York

They say to never make friends with your clients when you're a therapist. In fact, that's drilled in pretty hard at school. You need to be close enough to be able to help, but not so close that they consider you an actual friend. That way lies calls in the night, visits at home and unrealistic expectations. So I keep the tone formal.

My computer dings again.

Hi Keegan. Or Dr. York? Which do I call you? Wait, I didn't mean to start asking questions again. I just realized that it's past 10pm and I might be keeping you up with these emails, and if so, I'm sorry, because that's not my intention. I was just really happy you replied so quickly. So thank you, and sorry. I guess I already apologized, but you know how it goes. Sorry. God, I'm just going to stop typing.

Miranda

I don't think I've ever run into anyone who seems to literally type out what's in her head like that. Must be a speedy typist. And she's so keyed up, like she's afraid that if she stops typing, she'll bail out before daring to hit send. But she found my note at the club, so there's probably a BDSM angle to it. Or it might be completely unrelated. I don't know, but exchanging messages with her is fun.

Hi Miranda, and of course not. I just happen to be late in the office today. Don't worry about me. If I don't have time, I won't reply. I'll be here tomorrow. Have a good night.

Keegan

It's only just when I hit send that I realize I've already gotten more casual. Shit.

Ding.

Oh, thank you. I'm glad to hear it. Really stopping with the emails now. Sorry. Thanks. Have a good night.

Miranda

Well, now I'm definitely curious about what tomorrow's going to be like. Sounds interesting, to say the least.

3

KEEGAN

"So, why don't we start by finding out what you'd like out of these sessions?"

In one of my leather chairs, bought specifically for comfort to put clients at ease, sits Miranda Larson, watching me big blue eyes. Thick, blonde hair hanging down past her shoulders hints as much at her Scandinavian background as her last name does. Taller than average, with curves for miles and a full-lipped smile, she'd be the epitome of a sexy Valkyrie if her expression didn't look like the one of a mouse that just crawled into the food bowl of a hungry house cat.

Fuck, I'm not that scary, am I? From her emails, I expected more energy, but as soon as I came out to greet her, her eyes went wide and her face red. Suddenly getting words out of her is like pulling teeth. Doesn't make her any less easy on the eyes, though. In my mind, I know that getting all worked up about a client is both unethical and unprofessional, but it's not my mind that's fighting my brain for blood.

She swallows thickly, briefly meets my eyes and then drops her gaze. I don't think she's weak. It takes a good bit of bravery to work up to seeking help through psychotherapy, even when I call it coaching to make it seem more approachable. I get that. This isn't the first time I've had a nervous newcomer in my office.

"Take your time. We're in no rush." I set a cup down on the low coffee table in front of her. "Here you go. Cream? Sugar? Wait until you try it. This machine makes amazing coffee."

She nods, still not looking up. Everything about her body language screams help me, sparking my protective instincts. But I can't do that until she asks for it, or at least tells me what's wrong.

"Cream and sugar, please." She speaks into her lap, but it's a start. Could be worse. Like that client last year whose only words were hello when he came in and a mumbled goodbye when he left. It took several sessions before I finally got the poor guy speaking complete sentences.

"Sure." The coffee machine has a small refrigerator built into its side that perfectly fits a mug of cream. I appreciate little details. In my opinion, coffee is best black, but many clients prefer to soften theirs a bit. I bring it to the table along with a bowl of sugar.

She dumps two spoonfuls of sugar into her cup, making me wince, followed by enough cream to make her coffee run almost completely white. I'll have to refill the mug after the session. She's ruining a perfectly fine cuppa joe, if you ask me, but then again, she's not paying me to judge her coffee.

"Thank you," she mumbles, but doesn't drink.

Picking up my own cup, I ease back in the chair across from hers and take a sip. It goes down, black and hot, burning my throat, just the way I like it. No pleasure without pain.

"Would you like to get to know each other a little before we start?" She starts at my voice. "It can be difficult to bring up something personal with a total stranger. We don't have to jump out into the deep end right away—just test the waters a little."

Finally, she looks up, chewing her full lip nervously. It reminds me of a kind of look I like to see in a completely different type of session, but if I'm going to help her, I really need to push down how that makes me feel.

"I… I saw your ad at the club." She blushes and looks down again, as if it were disgraceful to even admit that she'd ever been there. Like a BDSM club is even a big deal these days. For some, I guess it still is. Not like I don't know that. I don't exactly advertise that I go there either, but she should know that she's in safe company. Hell, I'm surprised we haven't run into each other, given how many evenings I've spent there. Hasn't happened, though.

Trust me, I'd remember that.

I nod. "I'm glad. You're far from the first, and I think it's a field where I'm especially qualified to help. And while I don't know yet why you've come to me, I sincerely hope I can help you."

Gathering her courage, she raises her head and gives me a hopeful look. "So you've helped people like me before?"

"Like you? I don't know yet. I've helped many people. Sometimes the source of the issue doesn't matter. Sometimes it does. Everyone is different, so I can definitely say I've never helped anyone just like you before. But maybe I've helped someone relatable. Or maybe we're heading into an exciting new adventure together." I smile cautiously. Half expecting her to startle and run off like a deer come into my yard, I avoid making any sudden moves.

I get a wan smile back, which is a little victory.

"I don't know. This is stupid. I'm probably just wasting your time." Cradling her cup, she lifts it to her lips and takes a cautious sip. Apparently it meets with approval, since the next sip is deeper.

"Not at all. Anyone is welcome here." If nothing else, she could do with some help with her confidence.

"I feel guilty. And ashamed."

I frown. "Not about my time, I hope. I mean—"

"It's why I'm here." As if actually getting the words out gives her strength, she meets my gaze for real for the first time today. And what a gaze it is, her deep blue eyes fixing on mine with a surprising intensity. For a moment, I forget myself, like there's more to this moment than just a counselor and his client, but of course there isn't. That's not why she's here, and I should know better.

Her jaw's set in determination and her fingers grip the armrests of her chair, her knuckles whitening. That admission took a good bit of courage, as much as coming here in the first place.

"Of course." I nod, quickly settling into professional mode "Would you like to tell me more?"

She pauses, nods, and then draws her breath and releases it.

"Anything said here is confidential. I promise. Just you and me, and I don't judge. This is a safe space, no matter what."

For the first time, her face takes on a wry expression, rather than one of despair. "What if I did something criminal?" I catch a glimpse of the person I imagined from the emails, and I like that.

Cocking my head, I raise a curious eyebrow at her. "Did you?"

"You first."

"I said confidential and I meant it. If you did something criminal, I might advise you to turn yourself in, but I wouldn't report it."

She examines me closely, then nods. "Okay." Just the one word, but there's a sense of acceptance in it. She leans back in her chair, then slouches, her shoulders sinking and her head lolling back against the high chair back. Relaxing for the first time since she came in.

It might be too early for me to call it progress, but it's something.

"Would you like more coffee?" I ask, mostly to get her talking again.

"No. Thank you." She draws another breath, and does that lip chewing thing again. Then she blurts out, "I'm not sure I can live without BDSM."

I blink. "Okay. That makes sense." I smile encouragingly. "How do you feel about that?"

"I don't think I can live with it either. I'm damned if I do and damned if I don't. Does that make sense?"

"It's not an uncommon thought, but everyone's experience is different. Why can't you live with it?"

She sighs, sits up, and takes a sip before answering. "It makes me feel so guilty. Like, who in their right mind enjoys being spanked, or flogged, or tied up, or…" She trails off, blushing.

After enough of a pause, I say softly, "Lots of people. I do. Sometimes."

"But it's not right," she blurts out.

"Why do you think so?"

"It's…" She stumbles over her words, searching for the right ones. "Usually, I'm a strong woman."

With a smile, I ease back. "I believe you. You dared to ask for help. That requires strength."

"But when I see someone trapped, made to do things…" Her breathtakingly blue eyes fix on mine. "Dirty things. Sinful things… I want them done to me too. And that's not right."

"If everything's consensual, and the rules agreed on in advance, is it still wrong?" I've had this conversation many times, usually with skeptics, but never with someone who's already a part of the scene. Or at least it seems she is.

She licks her lips before responding. "My mother raised me by herself. I… wasn't exactly planned."

"I see where you get your strength from. Raising a child on your own isn't easy. Did you know your father?"

"He… I don't want to talk about him right now."

Interesting, but we don't have to tackle everything at once. "All right. We'll stick to your mother then."

She nods and reaches for her cup, but finds it empty.

"I'll get you another one."

"No, thank you." She gives me a hopeful look. "You don't have hot chocolate, do you?"

Luckily, my fancy machine is just as good at hot chocolate as it is coffee. Too sweet for me, but I'll happily serve it. When I set the cup on the table, she nods her thanks and takes a cautious sip. The way her face wrinkles when finding it too hot is adorable.

I keep a cold water pitcher next to the coffee machine for sessions, and pour her a glass. "Here, this'll help. Are you okay?"

She nods while waving a hand at her mouth. "Too greedy," she replies, sounding almost like she's just been to the dentist. I'll be okay. Thank you." She breathes out heavily with a rounded mouth, trying to channel cool air over her tongue.

"Drink." I hold the cup out to her.

She looks up, then nods and takes it. She closes her eyes when she drinks, and it looks like it helps. "Thank you," she says again as she puts her cup down.

I nod, leaning back in my chair with my espresso. "You were telling me about your mother."

"Right. God, this sounds just like visiting a shrink on TV, doesn't it? 'Tell me about your mother'," she says in a deep voice while making air quotes. She even laughs, just barely.

I laugh with her, happy to see her come out of her shell a little. "We can talk about something else if you want. If you think that's too stereotypical."

Then she sobers again. "No, I think maybe Mom's important. She's... a little weird. Maybe she should come see you too."

"How about we focus on you for now?" I smile, not wanting it to sound like criticism.

"Yeah. Sure. It'd be way too weird to share a counselor with her anyway. Anyway, she has some really specific ideas about what's right and wrong, in general and specifically for her little girl." She looks away, towards the window. "Life wasn't easy for us when I was younger, and I think it had a large impact on her. And through her, me, I guess."

"Would you like to tell me about these things?"

She shakes her head. "Not yet."

Taking a chance, I lean forward to put my hand on her knee. It's warm under my palm. Her head snaps up to look at me. "You're safe here. I prom-ise. It's just the first session and we have all the time you want to take, but the more you can tell me, the better I can help."

She nods. "I just need a little time to get used to this."

"Of course." I lean back, smiling encouragingly. "So, your mother, then. You're an adult now. Do you live with her?"

"No."

"But the guilt is still there."

"You don't know what it's like. I love Mom, I really do. She's put me ahead of everything, made me the center of her life, but I can't help how I feel. And I don't have anyone to talk to about it."

"Did you try her?"

She snorts. "Yeah, right. Would you talk to your mom about wanting to have kinky sex? A documentary about it came up on the TV once, and she shut it right off. Apparently BDSM is only for dirty deviants and misogynists."

Right. Figures. "Well, you have me."

"Can you tell me why it isn't wrong? I mean, I've read so much about it, about people in the lifestyle and casuals. Is it okay to submit to someone if it's only temporary, or am I only validating a world where women are objectified and mistreated?" Her big eyes look up at me, eager for an answer.

"That's a tough question. And the answer differs based on who's asked. In my opinion, no, but then I'm speaking from a point of privilege, aren't I? What about the other way around? Many men enjoy being dominated as well. How do you feel about that? Is it just as bad, or is it their just desserts?"

She shrugs. "I don't know. I've thought about that too, and I don't have a good answer. But in my mind, I'm the submissive." Now that's a statement that gets my brain working hard. Briefly, she brings her hand up to her mouth. "Wow, I don't know if I've ever said that out aloud before."

"No judgment, remember? Everything's confidential."

She nods. "Yeah, that's a little weird. Actually, can I say a few other things?"

"Of course."

"I want to be spanked." She clenches her fists and grins like she's just gotten a free pass to be naughty. "I want to be tied up. I want to be whipped. I want someone to grab me by the throat and make me theirs." She's not even looking at me anymore, just glorying for a moment in the freedom of no judgment.

Meanwhile, I do my best to keep control, because fuck, those kinds of words are hard to ignore, especially when they come out of a girl like Miranda. I don't even know what the deal is, since I've never had this problem before. Always distanced, always composed, but damn, if there isn't something about her that makes that impossible.

I shift in my chair uncomfortably, my cock going rock hard in my slacks. That'd leave a good impression, right? I'm supposed to be a goddamn professional.

"I want candle drips and flogger whips and… hey, that rhymed." She giggles, and then it's like she suddenly remembers she's not alone. Her face turns bright red as her eyes go wide in shock and both of her hands clasp over her mouth. "I've… I've never…" she mumbles through her fingers.

I smile awkwardly while thinking about bills to pay, hockey stats and that I have to take out the garbage today, trying to make my steel bar of a cock wilt under the power of my will alone. It's not easy with the way Miranda's tits rise and fall under her shirt as she breathes hard. Luckily, she seems too embarrassed to notice.

Clearing my throat, I lean forward, both to seem supportive and to make the inappropriate bulge in my pants less obvious. "It's okay. There's nothing wrong with expressing your feelings. They're you. I think we're making some progress already. That's pretty impressive for your first session."

"Really? I don't know. I just blurted out the most embarrassing things ever to someone I've barely met." Distress fills her expression again. "God, I'm so ashamed."

"Don't be." Something about her makes me want to put my arm around her to comfort her. Hell, there's something about the way she carries herself that begs for it, but as much as my instincts scream at me to go for it, I'm the professional here. Build trust through competence, because if she starts to see me as a friend, we're getting too close. I still want to, though.

She shakes her head, still in her hands.

"Listen, they're just thoughts. Things you said. Ways to express how you feel. Putting words to them puts you in a position to deal with them. Trust me, this is progress." It's so important that she doesn't close back up.

And hopefully comes back for more sessions. It's dumb, since just by being my client, she's already off limits, but I really want to see her again.

"Really?" Still shivering from excitement, she looks at me with big eyes that can only be described as hopeful.

"Definitely."

This time I do take her hand and hold it in a way meant to comfort. Her shivering calms and she gives me a cautious smile. She grips me back, her skin so damn soft. If this woman isn't a born submissive, I'll eat my fucking shoes. If I can help her accept herself, whoever is lucky enough to be with her after is going to be a happy man.

I spend the rest of the session like that, holding her hand while she talks loosely about her mother and even mentions her father a couple of times, but she skirts around the issue without getting to the meat of it. We can only expect so much in the first session.

I glance at the clock and wince. "I hate to say it, we're out of time. I'd be happy to keep going, but I have someone coming in fifteen minutes, and I need a little time to prepare. Besides, after an hour or so, it's often good to pause a little and reflect."

Yes. Pause and reflect. God knows I need to clear my head.

She nods, not exactly confidently, but I think she's feeling just a little bit more secure than when she came in. I hope so.

"Listen, let's set up a new time soon. Kent out front will be happy to help you with that. He knows my schedule better than I do." I smile crookedly. "Assuming you'd like to come back, but I hope so. I think we can do good things together."

She chews her lip nervously again, but the look she gives me is definitely a good sign. "Okay. I'll do that. Thank you."

"No, thank you for coming. I'm looking forward to working with you."

The smile she throws me as she looks over her shoulder on her way out is adorable. As I close my door with a last glance at Miranda's gorgeous ass, I'm praying Kent finds her a time slot ASAP.

4

MIRANDA

"My God, he's so freaking good-looking. I was too shy to even speak most of the time."

Amber laughs at me. Leaning against the back wall of the playroom at the club, we're waiting for the stage show to start. She's wearing a tiny leather dress, paired with heels bordering on stilt height. She's got better balance than me, that's for sure.

My dress is more vanilla, covering all the way to my knees, and my heels are sensible rather than attempting any height records. Amber keeps telling me I need to dress more sexy, more 'scene', whatever that means, but even that feels like I'm giving in too much, and then I spend the whole evening uncomfortable and just a little ashamed.

She pokes my shoulder.

"Huh?"

"I said, if you could try paying attention this time, that it must be difficult to get any coaching from a guy like that. I mean, if you can't even talk to him, how are you going to get anything out of your sessions, even if he is into the scene? On the other hand, maybe that's something else to explore? Maybe personal coaching of a different kind is what you need to open up a little, huh?" She grins, as wickedly and naughtily as only she can.

"Oh, come on, you know I can't do that. That's why I'm trying this coaching thing to begin with."

"I don't understand why this is so difficult for you, but I hope he can help you. If you want, I'll even let you borrow Eric to tie you up sometime. Just no hanky panky." She winks. "He is a married man after all."

I won't claim that the offer isn't appealing. Eric's a handsome man, but it'd feel weird, even if I could let myself get to that point, so I shake my head with a faint smile. "Thank you, but he's yours."

Cocking her head to the side, she smiles sympathetically. "Will you ever tell me? I mean, I understand that you're really conflicted about this, and it's not like we've been lifelong friends, but in the time I've known you, you've seemed so interested and invested in learning about life on the kink side of things. But the moment I suggest you join in, it's like a wall drops down. No pressure, but I think it's bothering you, and I hate seeing my friends bothered." She winks. "Unless it's hot and bothered, of course."

That brings out a laugh from me. She's got a point. Somehow, I started opening up to Dr. York —Keegan, maybe—yesterday, but I'm unable to do the same with someone who's been my friend for almost a year. Caution is great and all, but she's never given me any reason to suspect that she's anything but genuine. Both her and her husband.

I try to phrase it gently. "I guess I'm not quite ready to talk about it yet. But even if we haven't been friends that long, I really appreciate it. It's totally not you, I promise."

She doesn't look offended, which makes me glad. I'd hate for things to get weird between us. She's the only one I've really gotten to know around here, and definitely the only one I can talk to about kinky stuff. Well, other than my new therapist, I guess. That's a strange thought.

"Oh wow, check that guy out. Phew." Amber fans herself with her hand while her eyes follow someone in the crowd like a hawk tracking a chicken. "There're a lot of good looking guys around here, but you don't see many of his caliber."

Following her gaze, I crane my neck while looking for him. And then I spot who she's talking about, and literally feel the heat radiating from my face as I flush. "Um… that's my therapist."

"Get out." She says it almost automatically, her eyes never leaving him as he weaves his way through the crowd. Not this way, luckily.

"For real."

"Forget about therapy, babe. You need to land that guy before someone else does." Then she cuts a quick look in my direction, long enough to ask a machine gun barrage of questions before turning to find him in the crowd again. "He is free, right? Was he wearing a ring? Pictures on his desk? Mention a wife? Girlfriend?"

"No," I reply, maybe just a bit too emphatically. "And you're saying that like there's a world somewhere where that would work. He's my therapist. And looks like a model. Seriously. My odds are like zero, even if I were going for it."

"Don't you dare sell yourself short. You're super cute. I'd kill for straight, blonde locks like yours."

"It doesn't matter. Either he's my therapist helping me with my problems, or he's not and I still have all my hangups and there's no way it'd work out. Doomed either way." I blow a few strands of hair out of my face. "I bet he has all sorts of rules preventing him from getting too personal with his clients."

"Well, we're about to find out."

"Huh?"

"He's coming this way."

Oh my God. He is. And he's looking at me, and smiling that ridiculously handsome smile of his.

What do you say to someone that sexy? Like I wasn't tongue tied enough yesterday.

"Quick, let me hide behind you." I move in her direction, but she just laughs and steps away, leaving me looking very obvious and awkward.

"Nuh uh. This is your chance."

"I'm telling you, there is no chance."

"No chance of what?" That last voice is unmistakably his, deep and a little rough around the edges. His smile beams in my direction, and I'm standing here like a deer in headlights. "I'm sorry, I shouldn't butt in on a private conversation, but I saw you there, and wanted to say hi."

"Hi," I reply meekly. My face is turning the club playroom into a red light district all on its own.

Amber nudges me. "Aren't you going to introduce me to your friend?"

I send a killing glare her way, but she just grins at me, knowing exactly what she's doing. Since she refuses to drop over dead, I do the only thing I can do. "Amber, this is Dr. York. I just met him yesterday. Dr. York, this is my friend Amber.

Despite appearances, she can be really nice once you get to know her."

They shake hands, and something ugly rises inside me. Really? I'm jealous of her touching him first? Maybe I need more help than I thought.

"Just Keegan's fine," he says. Given our relationship right now, I'm not sure whether that goes for me too, or not. "Nice to meet you, Amber." And then he turns to me, and I don't see anything else in the club. Just him.

"Hi," I say again, hopefully with a bit more conviction this time.

"Enjoying yourself?" he asks. "After yesterday, I was surprised I'd never run into you here, and then what do you know? Here you are."

"Yeah." I giggle inanely. "Go figure."

He scratches the back of his head. "I mean, I suppose I might've kept an extra eye open, just to see how you're doing. All things considered."

"Sure. Yeah. All things considered." I can't tell if he's putting moves on me or if this is just plain awkward. "You have an extra eye?"

For a moment, he stops, looking at me like I'm crazy, then laughs before leaning in conspiratorially. Up close, he smells really good. He puts his hand on my shoulder, and while the touch shouldn't feel anything but casual, I can feel each finger burn my skin. He stage whispers, "Yeah, but you have to keep quiet about it. It's a secret."

Amber pipes up, completely forgotten by both of us. "Oh hey, that's my husband over there. I think I'll just... walk away and leave you two to talk. Obviously, you've got a lot to—"

"Wait, don't leave me." Faster than I'd think I was capable, I reach out to grab her wrist. No way is she leaving me alone with him in an atmosphere this charged.

Keegan takes a step backwards, though he's still got that sexy smile on. "It's all right. I've got some things going on tonight anyway. I'll leave you two to it." He speaks to both of us, but his eyes never leave mine. "And I'll see you on... Thursday, was it?"

I nod. "Yeah."

He gives a little wave, then walks off, disappearing into the crowd, leaving me wondering what exactly that was about. As a therapist, would it make sense for him to come over and talk to me in a casual setting like that? Was he here looking for me? If so, why?

Amber clutches my upper arm with both hands, bubbling over with excitement. "Oh my God, oh my God, you have to get with him." She's yelling so loud, I try to bring her back down on the ground, half afraid that even over the noise of the club, he's going to hear her.

"Shh. Jeez, Amber. The last time I saw you this excited was when Eric came by with glow-in-the-dark ropes."

"He's totally got the hots for you."

"What? No way. A guy like him? He was just being friendly. Just saw someone he knew."

Amber laughs right in my face. "God, Miranda, I swear you're blind as a bat. Didn't you see how he looked at you? How he completely ignored these curves?" She takes a step back and wiggles her butt while gesturing at herself. She grins. "They always at least look, especially when I wear this dress. That's part of the fun."

I'm not sure if I can deal with Amber like this, right now. "Listen, he can't, and we won't, because that's not the relationship we have." I say it as convincingly as I can, hoping that'll quiet my own thoughts as well.

She leans in close, closer even than Keegan when he whispered, and says a single word.

"Yet."

"Oh stop it." I shake my head, but I can't help laughing at the conspiratorial look on her face. She's so set on getting me hooked up and into the lifestyle, it's a little scary sometimes. "I don't even know what he's into. Even if I somehow decide to make the leap, what if he's into, I don't know... something really gross."

She glances at the crowd, obviously looking for him. "With a face like that? I'd take the chance. But I bet he'll tie you up, give you a solid spanking and then make you beg for more. That's what I think, anyway."

"You're crazy." I say that, but the tingle that rushes right through my gut to between my legs is so very, very real.

"And you're letting life pass you by." Her light-hearted teasing takes an exasperated turn. "Really, there's this wonderful world in here, and you obviously want to be part of it. I don't understand what's holding you back, but imagine this: you, in twenty years, looking back. Which you will it be? The one who wishes she'd dared to take a chance all those years ago, or the one waking up next to her sexy husband, eager to know what kinky and fun tortures he's going to put her through that day?" She crosses her arms and quirks an eyebrow. "I know what I'd choose. What I chose."

I'm a little taken aback by how strongly she's coming on. Amber's bubbly and not afraid to speak her mind, but even from her, that was pretty over the top. A part of me agrees with her, but the rest is feeling an anxiety attack coming on, like I'm slowly sinking into deep water and it's about to close over my head. I want to do what she says, but I can't, and I know it's not going to make any sense to her.

I shake my head. "I think I need to go."

"What?" She stares at me in confusion.

"I need to… think." Find myself some quiet, some solitude. Suddenly everything about the club, and the people and knowing that Keegan is out there, all feels too oppressive. "I'm sorry, Amber. I'll see you later."

"Wait." But she doesn't stop me, even if her eyes burn holes in my back as I rush out of the play area. I nudge my way through the packed dance floor in the main hall and get my coat from the coat check. The doorman, a huge guy in a black T-shirt stretched across his broad chest and with a clean-shaven head, steps aside with a smile to let me leave, then waves in a couple who're waiting in line.

It's not far to my beat-up Toyota that's stuck with me since high school. I slide into the driver's seat before locking all the doors. Then I sit there for a while, both dreading the next session with Keegan, and thinking it can't come quickly enough.

And if that isn't just a little scary, I don't know what is.

5

MIRANDA

When I arrive at Keegan's office, he's speaking with his receptionist in the front room. At the sound of the door, he turns and locks his jade eyes on me in a gaze of molten green. His smile makes my stomach flip and my knees all wobbly.

"Miranda." Keegan's deep voice is sex for the ears, but then his expression turns serious. "Are you all right? You look…"

"Tired? Yeah, I didn't sleep well. If you find me snoring during our session, just kick me."

He laughs softly, but his eyes are soft with concern. "Insomnia? Bad dreams?"

"Yeah, something like that." I hold my hand out in greeting instead of running away, warmed by a flash of pride for my daring.

Bad dreams? Try the worst nightmares I've had in a long time. I was still living at home, Dad was chasing me around the kitchen table with a belt, bellowing that he was going to give me exactly what a bad girl like me deserved. It never actually happened, at least not just like that, but he chased me around my dreams all night. When I finally rolled out of bed, it was as if I hadn't slept at all.

It's probably something good to discuss with a therapist, but I'm totally not ready for that.

Keegan takes my hand, then pulls me gently closer, putting his other one at the small of my back. He exerts a slight pressure, guiding me. "Well, let's go talk in my office. Maybe a cup of hot chocolate will make you feel better."

"That sounds nice." With a nod and a faint smile, I let him steer me into his office. Even through my coat, his touch is warm and insistent. A shiver tracks down my spine, making the rest of me shudder for one thrilling moment.

He takes my coat, his footsteps muffled by the soft carpet as he goes to hang it up on a rack in the corner. "I'm glad you came back. I was afraid you might change your mind after our last session."

"No, no, it was good. I was—" Scared out of my mind. "It was… enlightening. I think, maybe I learned some things about myself?" I'm not exactly the voice of confidence these days. Or any days, if I'm honest.

His left eyebrow arches and his grin goes crooked, giving him a skeptical look. "Really? Good to hear. That already has me looking forward to today's session. Why don't you have a seat?" He gestures towards the leather chair I used last time. "Ready for that hot chocolate?"

I smile gratefully. "Please."

He punches a button on a very professional-looking, burnished chrome coffee machine. It whirs, hisses and then fires a mixture of cocoa brown and milky white from two small spouts into a deep coffee mug. He sets a second mug up and punches another button, leaving the machine grinding while he carries the first one over to me. "Here you go. Remember, it's hot."

Nodding my thanks, I take a careful sip.

Ouch.

"You know, I should know better by now," I say around my burnt tongue. "I'm always too eager. I must be a glutton for punishment."

He laughs as he pours a glass of water and hands it to me. "Well, perhaps that comes with the territory."

I blush at the implication while sipping the cool water. It soothes my tongue, at least for the moment. I'll be feeling the burn all day, most likely.

He goes back to the machine for his coffee, giving me a couple of seconds to admire him from behind. He's wearing a suit, though the jacket is hung over the back of his chair. His white shirt is rolled up to his elbows, exposing powerful fore-arms, and his slacks hug his ass in a way that makes me jealous of them.

I would be the one to end up with the sexiest ther-apist on record. I blow over my hot chocolate to cool it, while trying to ignore the tingle at the tip of my tongue.

He returns with his coffee and eases into the chair opposite. Cradling the cup in his hands, he looks me over, and this gaze feels just a little more predatory than would seem appropriate in a typical doctor-client relationship. I shiver a bit, even though it's not cold at all. It's not a bad shiver, exactly. Excited, maybe? Anticipatory?

"So." He tastes the word briefly before continuing. "How should I take care of you today?"

"I... shouldn't you be the one deciding that?" Glancing over the top of my cup at him, I hope it hides what I imagine is the deep blush on my cheeks. He didn't mean that like it sounded—at least I don't think so—but that doesn't mean that my mind isn't going places very quickly. Sexy, scary places.

He wets his lips while he thinks, and I can't not follow his tongue as it moves. "I have some ideas, but I'm here for you. It's important that you tell me if there's something on your mind, or something you'd like us to talk about. Or do."

My mind quickly spins towards things I'd like him to do, immediately followed by a surge of guilt. He's my therapist. We're in a professional relationship, and I really should treat it that way. Those things I imagine him doing… I could never do that anyway.

"I… I don't really know, to be honest." I know what I want to say, but it sounds so much like what I shouldn't. But still I want to, so badly. I'm never going to come to a decision on my own, so I draw a deep breath and just say it. "I… I think maybe it would be best if you decide."

For a moment, just a moment, but I know I'm not imagining it, his facade cracks. His eyes close and his Adam's apple bobs as he swallows deeply and draws a deep breath through his nose. Then the man recedes and the therapist returns.

I should want him to be professional.

Right?

Keegan's smile comes off soft and friendly, and when he speaks, his voice is even and sympathetic, but there's an intensity that never leaves his eyes. They hone in me like emerald lasers, so hot they're smoldering. His words sound innocent enough, but they also feel like a prelude to something deeper. At least in my hopeful mind.

"Then that's what I'll do. I just want to be sure you feel you're being heard, and that you're comfortable with how we're proceeding."

Am I comfortable? The way he's looking at me makes me wonder if he can keep his professional distance, and definitely whether I actually want him to. All I know is that my heart's beating like it's trying to break out of my chest and my palms are getting damp. Clutching the hem of my skirt while leaning forward, I try to dry them off discreetly while I consider my answer.

In some ways it seems obvious. I keep torturing myself by going to the club and immersing myself in this lifestyle, but I never take that final step. I never dare. On my own, I never will. I realize that.

No one judges you as deeply as yourself.

Amber's question about where I want to be in twenty years comes flashing back, and suddenly I know. I don't want to live my life looking back and wondering what might've been or what could've been. One way or another, Keegan is here to help me face my own judgment.

For the first time since I met him, I meet his gaze confidently. "Just tell me what to do"

He nods, his mouth crooked into self-confident smile. Did he know what my answer would be before I did?

"Have you ever heard of exposure therapy?"

Maybe? I shake my head.

"It's sort of like a vaccine. The idea is to introduce you to the things that you're bothered by in ways that are non-threatening. Small steps, making them seem harmless, until you're used to them."

"Okay?"

"Imagine you're afraid of spiders."

I cringe and he chuckles. I've never been a fan, even if I know they do a good job of taking care of other insects around the house.

"Exactly, so say you're completely terrified, but we find ways to expose you to them. We might start with education, about all the good things they do, exactly how they work, how harmless most of them really are, and so on. Perhaps show you how to identify the ones that are actually dangerous."

I nod when he gives me a questioning look to make sure I'm keeping up.

"Right, so after a while, we might expose you to live spiders, but in a safe way, like they're in an aquarium they obviously can't get out of, at a distance, and so on. Neutralizing your fears a little bit at a time. It's always ramping up, but just at the edge of the subject's comfort zone, slowly expanding it. I've seen a subject go from not being willing to be in the same room as a spider to being comfortable with letting a tarantula hang out on her arm."

I blanch at the thought. Ew.

He laughs at my expression. "It's all right. One thing at a time. I won't be introducing any spiders."

"You better not."

"Hey, you did say whatever I wanted to do, right?" His teasing grin makes it obvious he's joking. "No spiders. I promise. But I think it might be a good approach for you." A brief pause.

"That is, if you want to become more comfortable with BDSM. This is why we need to communicate. If you'd rather I help you move away from your fascination with the lifestyle, we could do that too, but I don't think that's what you want."

Time stands still. He's offering to help. He can make me forget all about it, so I can go on and live normally. Or he can teach me to accept it.

For a moment, I think of what it would be like to be free of the guilt and the shame. I wouldn't spend my evenings pining at the club. I wouldn't feel like I was betraying Mom by wanting what I do. She might not know that I feel that way, but I sure do. But it'd mean giving up something that feels so much like a part of me.

"Would it be difficult?" I'm not even sure which choice I'm asking about.

He shrugs. "Either way will have its challenges, but I want you choosing what we do based on what you want, not on how difficult it is. In the end, staying true to yourself is what will help you find happiness."

I nod, considering. Staying true to myself. What's true? What do I want?

"You can think about it. Nothing says we have to start right now. Or that any decision is irreversible. We'll probably have to change things as we go along. It's always a process."

I know what I'm supposed to want, but as much as I try to deny it to myself, I also know that what I really want is not the same thing. Given the choice of trying to forget what I really want or learning to live with it, maybe embrace it even, what I need to do suddenly seems so obvious.

A resolve fills me. "No, I've waited long enough. I don't want to wait any longer." I can't give up something that is such a part of me. If Keegan can help me come to terms with it and accept it, then that's what I want. What I really want.

What I need.

"Help me be myself."

"Okay, you've got this. Ready to start?" I give Miranda a smile that I hope is encouraging.

She nods, but there's nervousness written all over her face. Her eyes dart back and forth, taking in the room like a skittish animal. She stands straight in the middle of my office waiting for the first command. We're going to start simple and then take it from there.

"You're going to be fine. Nothing weird is going to happen today, I promise"

She grimaces. "Easy for you to say."

I take a moment to watch her. She's pure temptation. Fuck, I'm in trouble and we haven't even
started. I'm supposed to be professional and
hands off? Dr. Hastings, my Ph.D. advisor, would
be chewing me out if he knew the kinds of
thoughts that are going through my head
right now.

"We'll do this just like in a proper BDSM
session."

"I don't see any gags or ropes." A hint of her
playful nature breaks through, a cautious smile,
though her eyes are wide. If she can get rid of her
challenges, she'll make a delightful sub.

Not mine, obviously, but some lucky bastard's.
Being kink positive is already a step too far for
some of my more conservative colleagues. I know
how it would look to an ethics board if I'm caught
first helping a client to be subservient, only to take
her on as mine after the treatment is officially
ended. Grooming they'd call it, and I'd lose my
license immediately.

I shake my head. "No need for those. Not today,
anyway." If at all possible, her eyes widen just a
little further at that. Shit. Baby steps.

I move on before she can dwell too much on things that may or may not happen. "For now we'll run with standard safewords. If it becomes too much and you can't continue, call out red, and if something's not right, but not critical, call out yellow and we'll figure out how to change things so that you're okay. Sound good?"

Her expression fixed in concentration, she nods.

"Repeat it to me."

"Red means stop. Yellow means pause and change."

"Good. Arms out."

"What?" She frowns.

"We've started. Arms out."

She blinks. Then slowly lifts her arms until they're stretched out at her sides, hands flat and palms down. "Like this?"

"Good. How are you doing?"

She faintly shrugs. "I'm okay. All you did was ask me to put my arms out."

"But I didn't ask. I ordered you to. How does that make you feel?"

Pausing like she's tasting something new, she shrugs again. "I don't know. Not much. It doesn't really feel like much. It's more like doing you a favor, I guess?"

"Okay, good. Stand on one leg."

A faint smile forms on her lips. "Getting a little silly, isn't it?"

"Stand on one leg." This time my voice is harder, deeper. More like the voice I'd use in a scene.

Her leg snaps up, and even she looks a little surprised at how quickly it does, before she gathers herself. "I feel a little like Karate Kid here."

"Watch it, or I'll make you do a crane kick next," I tease. She giggles briefly at that, then starts to wobble. "Keep steady," I command and she responds, finding her balance again. Good. At least she's not freaking out. This is starting better than I thought it would.

It should probably bother me how much I'm enjoying this, even these stupid little commands.

Just watching her move at my whim gets me thinking about other ways I'd like to have her moving, and none of them are appropriate.

But the thoughts are inevitable.

"Put your leg down."

She does.

"Crouch."

She does that too, but a bit reluctantly. It's definitely a more vulnerable pose. I have to be careful. I want to challenge her, but not push her too hard.

"Kneel."

It takes a moment, but then she shifts forward until her knees are on the floor and her round ass is resting on her heels. My mind whirs, imagining her in that position without clothes on. Fuck. My dick is getting hard, and how the hell do I keep her from noticing?

"Eyes on the floor."

This time she swallows, but she bends her neck so she's looking down and not at me. It solves my immediate problem, but seeing her in such a submissive pose doesn't exactly make anything soften.

"Are you all right?" Just because she's turning me on, doesn't mean I can push her too far.

"Yeah." Her voice is a whisper, barely audible.

"There's no shame in using a safeword. Just let me know."

She nods, faintly, but doesn't say anything more. Just waits for my commands.

"Hands on your ankles."

This time there's no hesitation. I approach slowly, not wanting to spook her, until I'm standing right in front of her. The power imbalance is thick in the air, but even so, she's still.

So am I. I wait, letting the unevenness of our positions sink in. Let her think about it for a bit. Let her feel that right now, she's in my power. I can see all of her, but all she sees is the top of my shoes. In this position, I can watch her, how she's waiting for my next words. Her back rises and falls in time with her breathing. It's not labored, but definitely coming a little fast. She's not as calm as she'd like to have me think.

It puts me in a difficult situation. The principle idea is to not expose her to more than she can handle, to ease her into accepting and taking control of the feelings that are keeping her from doing the things she so desperately wants to do. Meanwhile, every nerve in my body is urging me to coax her further, to push her right up to her limits. I want to give her the excitement of going further than she thinks possible and luxuriate in seeing her squirm and fight against me until her inevitable surrender.

Needless to say, what I want and the proper procedures of the therapy are strictly at odds right now, and neither my big head nor my little head are particularly happy about the situation.

If she weren't looking down, I might even get a glimpse of cleavage, but given the state of my cock right now, I'm pretty sure having her look up isn't much of an idea. Fuck, she looks delicious like this, submissive and needy of what I have to give her. But I won't. She's not ready, and if she could hear my thoughts right now, then forget about safewords. She'd be out that door like a rocket and there'd be a lawsuit coming my way faster than you could say "red".

I take a step back before I'm too tempted.

"Spread your knees."

She hesitates. Just a moment, but she does, before settling into a perfect position of submission. The only thing missing is her wrists and ankles cuffed, making her completely helpless. I'd love that, as a matter of fact, but I'm not going to act on it. Jesus, why is this so hard? I've never had such a hard time staying in control of myself. I'm a damn professional, and I can act like it, even if my client is a gorgeous submissive.

Maybe I should back off, stop the session. I could do with some time to cool off. I glance at the time. Still twenty minutes of play left, where I try to not act like an animal. There's just something about her that makes it impossible to stop.

Shit.

"Down onto all fours."

This time, I can see the wheels spinning in her head. Where does the line between BDSM therapy end and true submission begin? That last command might just have crossed Miranda's line.

She confirms it when instead of moving, she says in a timid voice, "Yellow."

Well, at least it wasn't red. "Are you alright? What aren't you comfortable with?" Like I don't have a pretty good idea.

"I'm fine. I just… I'm not sure I can manage too much more of… well, this."

"Talk to me. What do you mean by this? The position? Is the floor too hard? Something more specific?"

With a resigned expression, she looks up. I immediately crouch down to be at her level, both so we're talking face to face, and so that my crotch isn't the only thing she sees.

She frowns. "It's… I don't know. I need to stop, but I don't want to. It's like having a devil and an angel on my shoulders. The angel keeps yelling at me, "What are you doing? Get up! Don't let him boss you around like that," while the devil tells me that this is what I wanted all along. That I need this." She lets go of her ankles to throw her hands out in a gesture of exasperation. "But even if I do, I can't let go of the feeling that this is dirty. Unnatural. Wrong." She sighs. "God, I'm such a mess. How the hell am I supposed to ever get to somewhere normal, when I'm torn like this?"

The first sniffle catches me unaware, but then a tear pops out of the corner of her eye and I react instinctively. Wrapping my arms around her, I pull her close and let her cry into my chest. Fuck, she fits right into my arms as if she were born to be there.

"Hey, it's okay, Miranda. Sometimes there are a lot of bottled up emotions that come out during these sessions. Take it easy. We're done for today, okay? No more commands this time." I pat her back. "You're going to be fine, and I'm here to watch over you."

In response, she snuggles closer against me while I do my best to provide a haven that feels safe. Working with Miranda is obviously going to bring up a lot of emotions, and she needs to learn that I might push her boundaries sometimes, but I'll never ask for more than she's willing to give.

She mumbles something, but her voice is muffled against my shirt, and I can't make it out.

"What was that?"

"I'm sorry." She turns her head so her mouth isn't covered. "I didn't mean to blubber all over you like this. I'm stronger than that."

Unable to help myself, I run a hand through her hair, stroking to comfort her. "Don't worry about it. I don't mind. Working with emotions isn't easy. It's like a good BDSM session. Sometimes it's painful, and difficult, but afterwards we feel better for it."

"Stop sounding so sensible," she mumbles. The crying seems to have passed, but she's still pressed firmly against me. I don't really want to let her go, and I don't think she wants me to either. So we sit there comfortably wrapped in each other's arms.

"I'm not sure sensible has ever been a good way to describe me, but I try." I chuckle dryly. "How are you feeling?"

"Better, I think."

"Good. Ready to stand?"

"I don't know. Am I allowed to?" she asks with a wry note in her voice. It's good to hear.

"The session ended with your safeword. You're free to do whatever you please."

"Okay."

Sometimes I'm slow, but it doesn't exactly pass me by that she's not standing, but still leaning into me. I laugh. "Maybe not whatever. As much as I'd love to stay like this, I do have another appointment coming up." I don't want her to leave. Fuck, I can't get attached like this. "Okay, up we go." Hooking my hands under her upper arms, I pull her up with me.

"Thank you." She smiles softly up at me.

"Any time."

"No, I mean for the whole session. It scared me a little, and it made me feel some uncomfortable things, but I think it might've helped. At least a little."

"Well, I'm glad, though I'd be careful about rushing things. Your wants and your conscience are in a bit of tension right now. It can snap back, in either direction. Spend a little time thinking, and do some relaxing things this weekend, and then we'll see how it goes next session."

She stands up straighter, her burgeoning confidence showing in spite of my warning. "Yeah, okay. That sounds good. When can we do that?"

"After the weekend, but you'll have to talk to Kent for a specific date."

"Got it." She opens the door before looking back at me over her shoulder. There's more than just goodbye in that look, but I can't quite decipher it. She smiles. "So, until next week then."

"Yep. I'll see you then. Unless we meet at the club, I suppose."

Her cheeks flush pink. "Right. Yeah. Well, I'll see you later."

I smile and nod. "I look forward to it."

For a moment longer we stand there, looking at each other before we both laugh.

"Get out of here," I say with a grin.

"Bye." She grins back and then she's out of my office.

Holy fuck, how am I going to keep this going? She's going to be the death of me at this rate. What a sweet way to go, though. I already can't wait for the next session.

MIRANDA

"Hello?"

"Miranda, there you are!"

Crap. I should know better than to pick up my phone without checking who's calling.

"Hi Mom. How are you?"

"I'm wonderful, actually, thank you. The sunrise was beautiful this morning, not that I imagine you were up to see it." The chide is gentle, but always there. Always little barbs. After nineteen years of being made to get up at dawn or close enough to it, I don't think it's too much to enjoy the freedom to sleep in when I can, but to Mom, that's already wasting the day.

"I'll have someone record it for me next time, all right?" The deep sigh at the other end is response enough, and I can't quite keep the smirk off my face.

"I do worry about you, lazing the day away like that. How are you paying for your apartment?"

"I started a new job over a month ago. I thought I told you. I'm working at a cafe."

"That doesn't sound very safe." My phone veritably oozes disapproval. Right, that's why I hadn't told her. "Who knows what kinds of men come by there? I certainly hope you don't work in the evenings. This is why I don't like you living in the city. Gladys and Debbie keep telling me that I should have you come visit more often. They miss you at the church group, you know."

"To be honest, I worry a lot more about entitled moms with baby carriages, barging through as if they own it the place. It's in a mostly residential area and pretty quiet as cafes go." I try to steer her towards a less dangerous topic. To Mom, every man is a probable enemy. It might be natural given her history, but I can't let it steer my entire life. "Besides, you've taught me to defend myself. I'll be okay. But tell Gladys and Debbie hi and that I miss them." In a 'miss them from afar but glad I'm not there' sort of way.

"Of course, but I really would love for you to visit."

I roll my eyes. Mom might be an imposing figure, but so long as I can keep her at a distance, it's not so bad. It makes it possible for me to do stuff like see Keegan, and maybe shake some of the many complexes she's gifted me with over the years.

"So what are you calling about anyway? It's great to hear from you, but it's rarely without a reason."

"What do you mean, what am I calling you about? I told you I'd give you a call when I was about an hour away so you have time to prepare."

"An… hour… away?" I swallow thickly, an icy sensation of terror crawling slowly down my spine, leaving trail of goosebumps as it progresses. "Wait, you're… coming here? Now? Like, today?"

"Don't you check your messages?" There's a clearly exasperated tone to her sigh, as if I mess this up all the time.

"What kind of message? Facebook? Phone? Letter? Carrier pigeon? I don't remember seeing anything."

"You know I don't get that internet stuff. I left a message on your voicemail."

Figures. Other than my mom about once a year, the only ones who leave messages there are the occasional phone sales robot that thinks I picked up when it hears my voice. I check it like once every couple of months.

"I guess I missed it. I'm sorry." Crap, crap, crap. "It's not a problem. I just need to… tidy up a little." I glance around my mess of an apartment. Not just messy, but there're BDSM toys all over my bedroom. I might not dare to practice, but Amber keeps taking me shopping and I've acquired more than my share of weird stuff, even if I've never dared to mess with it. Stuff that Mom would freak if she saw. "You know you're always welcome."

Technically yes, of course. I love Mom. But man, her timing is just never good. Sometimes I think she does it on purpose.

"Of course. I'll hang up then and give you time. We'll talk when I get there."

"Sure thing. Love ya, Mom."

"Love you too, sweetie."

My anxiety, not at all insignificant on its own, shoots through the roof. Everywhere I look, I spot things that are going to rat me out, generate questions, or just flat out be disapproved of. So much for going to the club tonight. And how am I going to explain my therapy sessions? How long is she even going to be here? And why?

So many questions, and only some of them will have easy answers. Meanwhile, I'd better shake a leg if I want my apartment in shape for the Mom invasion.

How come nothing ever is as simple as it should be?

Miranda definitely said she was going to be here tonight, but I haven't seen any signs of her. I've been back and forth across the play area three, four times already. I even checked the dance floor a couple of times and once up by the bar. Ran into Gabe and that massive partner of his, Caleb, but other than that, no familiar faces.

I've got it bad.

What happened to not fraternizing with my clients? To be fair, this is the first time my client has been as drop dead sexy as this one. And gets me firing on all plugs like she does. It's bad enough that I have to stay professional during our sessions. I was hoping to see her at the club where we could be more relaxed, and the disappointment is killing me.

"Hey, Doc." The voice is bright, cheery and off to my right. When I turn my head, I find Brandy— no, that's not right—maybe Brianna… Fuck, how am I supposed to remember Miranda's friend's name when Miranda was standing right there, distracting me when we were introduced? Amber. That's it. I raise my hand in greeting.

"Hey there. How's it going?" So technically, I shouldn't be asking about Miranda, right? I can't help myself anyway. "Having a night out without Miranda?"

She frowns. "Yeah, don't remind me. She had to cancel last minute."

Hopefully it's not because of our session. It got a bit tense there. "Is she all right?"

"Physically, sure."

"But…"

"Her mother's in town. Apparently Miranda missed the message or something and barely got her toys stashed away in time." She winks, as if it wasn't obvious what kinds of toys she's talking about.

But if her mom's in town… "How long is she going to be here?"

"She didn't say." She smiles and looks at me with a knowing expression on her face. "You seem very curious about someone who's just a client. There isn't more to it, is there?"

"Of course not. I'm just hoping that it doesn't mess up the scheduling for her next appointment is all." That sound evasive enough? The glint of amusement in her eyes makes me suspect I'm not fooling anyone. "It's always a hassle to squeeze in a replacement for an open slot at the last minute."

"Uh huh. Right. I'm pretty sure that's not what you want to squeeze into."

I clear my throat, coughing to cover up my reaction to her bluntness. Apparently I'm a lot more obvious than I think. "I don't comment on my relationships with my clients."

At that she bursts out laughing. "You're lucky I'm already married, Dr. York. Otherwise Miranda would have some competition." Then she stops and her expression turns serious. "Miranda is my girl, okay? You be nice to her. She's obviously got difficulties accepting who she is, and I bumble along trying to help her through it, but you're a professional. I hope you can make her feel better, but don't take advantage of her or I will cut you. Is that clear?"

Whoa. My first instinct is to laugh, but her expression is dead serious. "Listen, you're a great friend for protecting her, but honestly, as her therapist, I can't have any kind of relationship with her other than professional. The only reason I'm even admitting to her being my client to you, is because I know she already told you."

"Sure, but you want to have more than a professional relationship with her, don't you?" Her teasing smile comes back. "I'm not blind."

I shrug. "It doesn't really matter. My first objective is to help her. I'm not going to mess things up just because I find her attractive."

"Hah! So you do find her attractive." Her grin widens.

"Not the point."

"It totally is the point." She grabs my arm as if I'm about to bolt. "Miranda needs someone. Maybe it's you."

"She's a strong woman. I'm just helping her sort through some things."

"I still think she needs someone. And I worry about her mother being here. I don't know if Miranda's mentioned it, but she's a bit… controlling." She curls her lip briefly.

"I can't really comment on that."

"Well, she's probably terrified that her little girl isn't living up to the family ideals. Which, in this case means her ideals. If her mom knew anything about this place, or that Miranda likes to come here, she'd go ballistic."

I make a non-committal noise, uncomfortable with the way this conversation is going but wanting the insight Miranda's friend might provide.

"You have no idea. I was at Miranda's place once, and overheard a phone call. That was bad enough. Even over the phone she was trying to micromanage her daughter, who's freaking twenty-two. Time to let your kid fly, you know?"

I nod. There's obviously more to it than just micromanagement, but I need to cut things off before this gets out of hand. "Listen, I appreciate your input, but I can't talk about this with you. Miranda needs to be able to trust in my confidentiality."

"Good, right, so we'll just talk as friends. We can do that, right? I know something's bothering her, but I don't want you to tell me. I can guess, but if she wants me to know, she'll say." She pauses and thinks. "But, just as a friendly suggestion, I think you should take her out. Maybe I can deflect her mom for a while."

"Take her out? Did you miss what I said about keeping things professional?"

"I've seen how you look at her, even just the other evening. She doesn't dare jump into participating in the games here for her own reasons, but you're holding back from her in the exact same way. Isn't it better if you do what you actually want to do, and not just wish you did?"

It's tempting, but I'm already deep into unethical territory just by thinking about it. Inappropriate relations with a client is the number one reason for therapists losing their license, and she's my goddamn client. She needs to be able to trust me. And I need to be able to trust myself with her.

It's not just the fear of losing my license, or jail time, it's the damn principle of it all.

"I don't think that'll be possible, unfortunately. I have to do this by the book, as much as I can. But I do appreciate your input."

She grins. "I think you're making a mistake. It wouldn't take much to have her begging for your input, if you know what I mean."

And Amber claims Miranda's mother is controlling. I try to keep my expression neutral. "I think it might be best to leave the therapy to me, and let me help her the best way I can see how."

She rolls her eyes, but it's with a smile. "Oh fine. Do it your way. I bet you have diplomas and books and stuff that say that my way isn't the right way, but sometimes all someone needs is the right human contact. That's all I'm saying."

"And in a situation where it wouldn't create an ethical dilemma, those are wise words. She's lucky to have you as a friend, but don't go so hard on her, okay?"

"I don't go hard on her. If it was up to me, I'd already have her tied up and flogged until she admitted that that was exactly what she wanted."

"And that's why I'm the one with the diplomas," I say with a wink.

"Oh, fine," she responds with a mock pout. "Are you going to check out the demos? Gabe and Dawn are making their big comeback after their kid was born. No rough play while she was pregnant."

"Sounds sensible, but I just realized I've got some things to do. I'll catch them next time. Gabe always does good work."

She nods. "Oh, yes he does. Anyway, there's my husband. I'll see you later, then." She rushes off towards the stage area, leaving me to find my own way out, which is fine.

Much as I hate it, I need to dial it back a bit with Miranda. There are plenty of guides on what to do when you find yourself falling for your client. Usually it involves recommending them to someone else and removing yourself from their lives. Definitely not encouraging it, since a client-therapist relationship will never be on even ground. I'm finding it really hard to consider that right now, but I can't fuck this up for her. She deserves better than that.

So when I'd rather take her into my arms and kiss her silly, I'll stick to the therapy plan.

Doesn't mean I have to like it, though.

9

KEEGAN

"I wasn't sure you were going to make it today."

I smile as Miranda enters my office and closes the door behind her. The sun coming in through my window lights her up, giving her a soft yellow halo. Like an angel. Every so often, as the boughs of the oak outside move in the breeze, they casts dappled shadows on her, bathing her in a patchwork of dark and light. I have to blink it away as she settles into her chair and I'm reminded this is another regular session.

Well, as regular as they get when Miranda is here.

She smiles awkwardly. "Mom thinks I'm at work. I feel terrible for lying."

"Well, to be totally up front, your therapy is none of her business unless you choose to include her. I think a white lie here and there isn't too dangerous." I start the machine to make hot chocolate while giving her a searching look over my shoulder.

"Yeah, I guess so." She doesn't sound completely convinced, but I let it pass.

"It's for the best, at least until you're ready to talk to her," I say and hand her the mug. "Don't forget, it's hot."

"Oh yeah." She was already raising it to her lips, eager for her dose of creamy sweetness. It's amazing how excited she gets about hot chocolate, especially when it's just out of a machine. Maybe one day I'll make her some from scratch. It'll blow her mind. Except that I can't, not if I want to remain detached.

It's turning to out to be much easier in theory than it is in practice.

She licks her lips. "So what's the plan today?"

I sit down with my black coffee and try to make my expression as placid as I can. If nothing else, so I won't look like a wolf pacing around a sheep's pen. "How are you feeling after last week? Was it too much?"

"What? No." She pauses, then a faint tinge of pink flushes her face. "Well, maybe a little. But progress is bound to be a little uncomfortable, right?"

"Yes, sometimes. But I don't want to push you too quickly."

"I don't think you are." The words fall out of her, coming quickly. "In fact, if we could maybe do some of that again? I promise I won't spook as easily."

I look at her intently, trying not to get too distracted by how beautiful she is. And brave, facing her fears like this. Trusting me. My jaw tightens. "That's a bit of the point. I don't want you getting spooked, and if you really feel that it's too much, I don't want you to not call out your safeword just for my sake." I swallow, remembering how goddamn sexy she looked on her knees. What about this made me think that I could do it without being affected, exactly?

"Remember, I'm just here to help you. We take this at your pace."

It's funny. The first time she came in here, she was the one nervous and looking away. Today, I want to do the same thing. She's temptation in the flesh, and I'm supposed to ignore it and give her the help that she wants. That she needs. Rather than making her mine, which is what I really want to do.

Her voice takes me out of it. "Are you okay?"

"Who? Me?"

"Yeah, you. You seem… I don't know. If I didn't know better, I'd say nervous."

I laugh softly, trying to make it sound natural. "I'm worried that you're pushing harder than you should. Maybe this time—"

"I'm fine." It's the most confident I think I've ever heard her. "I trust you."

Those three little words, and I feel like I've already betrayed them, just by thinking of the things I want to do to her. I draw a deep breath. I can do this. I've counseled plenty of people in the lifestyle and there's no reason Miranda should be any different.

I pick up my notepad, holding it like a professional shield against the impulses she probably doesn't even know she's causing. "Good, but I still have some questions. How do you feel about last time?"

"What do you want to know?"

"What did you like? What didn't you like? What can I do to make you feel safe while we practice?"

"I…" A deep flush creeps up her neck and floods her cheeks. "I liked when you ordered me around. Even if it was stupid stuff, there was… I don't know, a kind of freedom in it. I didn't have a choice because you were in charge, and it didn't matter whether I had a problem with it or not."

I nod. "True. A lot of people feel that way about submission. It lets you be free to enjoy what you feel you shouldn't, but even if you enjoy it in the moment, the shame and guilt might hit you twice as hard afterwards. After all, the submission is, ultimately, your choice. When lifestylers claim that it's really the submissive who's in charge, they're not too far off the mark. You decide when it starts, when it stops, and how much is too much. Otherwise it's not BDSM, it's abuse."

"Yeah. I mean, I know the theory of it. God knows, Google is probably sick of me at this point." She pauses with a little smile. "Either that, or there's some employee there getting a kick out of my endless list of kinky searches."

With a laugh, I take a sip of my coffee before it gets too cold to be good. "I doubt that you're anywhere near the extreme of what they've seen. Remind me to tell you about Rule 34 sometime."

She draws her face into a very skeptical sort of grimace, her mouth turning down and her chin pulling back. " 'If it exists, there's porn of it.' Already aware of it, thank you very much. No need to go down that route. Like I said, I've Googled a lot."

"So, how did you feel after our last session? Once you had some distance."

"Honestly? I felt elated. Like I'd dared to do something that's part of me, even if it was something so basic and simple."

"No guilt?"

"Oh, there was guilt. A little later. I got home, flopped onto my couch and starting questioning what on Earth I'd done." She flops her head back against the headrest. "I'd been a bad girl, or at least it felt that way."

The way she says 'bad girl' makes my therapy instincts tingle. "Maybe it's time we take a closer look at where this comes from."

She looks about as excited as the time I started talking about spiders. "Do we have to?" she whines.

"You're not getting bratty with me, are you, sub?" I intended for that to come out jokingly, but it must've been sterner than I thought, because she shakes her head immediately and straightens in her seat.

"No, Sir."

Instinct kicks in. "Good, because avoiding the important subjects won't help us make progress. What has given your mother such a hold on you?"

She looks away. "My father."

I remain silent. Now that she's begun, I'll let her take it at her own pace.

"He… hit Mom. Like, a lot." Her face tightens, and my heart aches at the obvious pain the memories bring with them. "She was black and blue just… all the time. Fists, belt… He had a bamboo rod hanging on a hook in the kitchen. He loved to say that it was thinner than his thumb, so she had nothing to complain about." She swallowed. "Never above the neck, though, or anywhere it could be seen. He wasn't that dumb."

Shit. I suspected something like this, but still, shit. "How old were you?"

"When we ran away? I was ten. But it started before I can remember. Mom said he used to be nice. At least until she got pregnant. He was an executive on the rise and she was barely out of high school, trying to figure out what to do with herself. Her family had no money for college or stuff like that so I think he always thought she was beneath him. They met at a bar and he smooth talked her into bed, and things happened." She gestured to herself. "He insisted on doing the right thing, and married her, but we would've been better off without him. I think he hated the life he ended up with, and little by little he started to take it out on us."

"I'm sorry."

She gives me a wan smile. "Mom's told me the story several times. I saw him at his worst and was too young to remember the good times, but she wanted me to know how insidious it was. Sharp words at first, maybe a bit of a nudge or grabbing her a bit too hard. Enough to make her feel like it would stop if she just was a better wife or mother. By the time I was old enough to understand what was happening, she'd spend all her time trying to make sure he wouldn't get angry, but it was never enough." She shakes her head, as if trying to clear herself of the memories, then sniffles. "And it wasn't just words anymore."

There's a ton of literature arguing against what I'm about to do. I'm a counselor, not a friend. Or something more. But I can't help it, not when she's like this. I stand and walk to her chair. She looks up, her beautiful blue eyes shining.

Kneeling down by her chair, I wrap my arms around her and pull her close. She resists for barely a second before she eases into me, her face against my chest and her arms around my waist.

"I'd hear it at night, after she'd put me to bed," she forces out, her voice strained. "The yelling, the screams, it was horrible. I never saw it. Well, almost never, but what made Mom finally break away was when he hit me. It only happened once. He'd threatened me tons of times, but one day he was in a particularly bad mood and I guess he thought I was big enough to take it. It wasn't even hard. Nothing like what he'd do to her. I was more surprised than anything, but Mom told me later that was the moment she realized it wasn't going to stop. He was going to do it to me too." She shudders, and I squeeze her harder.

"The next day, while he was at work, she packed all of our clothes into two suitcases, called a cab and we were out of there. Not just our house, but out of town. She got a neighbor to help book us plane tickets across country to get back to my grandparents. I found out later that Dad came looking for us, but Grandpa chased him away with his shotgun. Other than receiving the signed divorce papers in the mail, it was the last thing we ever heard from him." She's silent for a while, before she whispers nastily, "Coward."

We're both quiet for a long time. She needs time to think more than she needs my advice right now, and I'm not going to push her out of my arms. Not ever. Putting a hand in her hair, I stroke it gently. "How are you feeling?"

"Right now? Better than I thought, to be honest." She snuggles closer into my chest. "I haven't talked about this to anyone in... I don't know, forever. Mom and I would talk about it, a little, but mostly I was brought up with the evils of men up front and center. She never moved on after we left. Her church and the friends she made there have become her whole life. Mom knows, and I guess I know, that Dad was a bad man. Most men aren't like that, but he wasn't always like that either. How do you separate the good ones from the bad?"

"There is no simple test, unfortunately, but I can teach you some red flags to look for. I'm amazed you're talking to me at all. Why didn't you try a female counselor?"

"I did. A few years ago. We got started, and then I mentioned that I had an interest in kink, and she grew convinced that it was a counter-reaction to what I'd experienced and that I needed to be cured of it. That it obviously was something wrong with me, and not just... well, what it is."

I shake my head, upset that Miranda's had to live with her problems for longer than necessary, but I can't regret that she's in my life now. "Sometimes you just find the wrong counselor."

Finally, she leans back and looks up at me. There's a little smile back on her lips. "And sometimes you find the right one."

She looks so certain that all I want to do is to hold her close and keep her safe. Protect her, and help her break away from the hold that lowlife piece of shit father put on her. As a counselor, that's my job, but I can't deny that it runs deeper than that, and this is quickly becoming more than a simple doctor-client relationship.

I'm going to have to tread really carefully.

10

MIRANDA

I see him the moment I enter the club. His back is turned, but I'd know that shape anywhere. He's wearing a black suit, and the way it tapers from his broad shoulders towards his narrow waist gives him a shape that's so sexy, it should be illegal. Already, I hate that I'm not the only one here who gets to look at him.

Calm yourself, woman, this is a session, not a date. And it's only been two days since I saw him last.

He turns, and the way his face lights up sure makes it feel like a date, though. "Miranda, you're here. Good." He takes my hand, not quite pulling me to him, but closer, so it's easier to talk over the rumbling bass of the dance music. "Are you ready for this?"

After the emotional outpouring of our last session, his suggestion to make the next session something a little more physical and cathartic made sense. A bit of a break, and a chance to try the exposure thing again, this time in a more appropriate setting. At least it made sense at the time. Now that I'm here, with the music pounding and the knowledge of what sorts of things go on in the play area at the other side of that tunnel, it feels as intense as our session was.

So am I ready? I don't know. Do I want to get better? Definitely. So I nod and smile up at him. "Let's do this." And then, after a moment's consideration, I tack on, "Sir."

Those sexy green eyes of his narrow, and his smile curls up on one side, giving him a very predatory look. Like the big bad wolf.

Is he going to eat me?

Oh God, I can't believe I even thought that. Hopefully it's too dark in here for him to notice my flush.

"I've booked us a private room where we can practice. Are you okay with that?"

The private rooms are the only part of the club where I've never been. Well, those and the men's room, I guess. I've been insanely curious, but never had reason to enter. It feels like a commitment of sorts, but I trust Keegan, so I nod. "Yes, that's fine."

He leads me past the dance floor, clearing space through the undulating throng, so that we can pass. Then we head down the tunnel that separates the dance floor from the play area, emerging out on the other side with only a faint thumping sound remaining from the music behind us. The rush I always get when visiting this part of the club isn't made any less with the knowledge of what we're about to do.

We walk past the public scening, full of naked people, bound people, completely enclosed in leather or latex people, whipping people and on and on until we get to the private rooms.

I draw a nervous breath. "So here we are."

Pulling a key card out of his pocket, he goes straight towards the closest one. "This is ours." He gestures for me to enter. "After you."

"Thank you, Sir." I step inside, and see one of the rooms for the first time. Everything is black. The floor, the walls, even the ceiling, though there are hidden lights giving an indirect glow all around the ceiling.

There's so much to look at. Whips on one rack—floggers, crops, a bullwhip, all ready for use. On another hangs rope in different lengths and thicknesses, a selection of sizes of leather cuffs, and whole bunch of metal restraints like spreader bars and portable stocks. It's a kink smorgasbord. All of those are things I've studied the hell out of, but few that I've ever been close enough to see and touch.

"Does it meet with your approval?" Keegan's amused voice brings me back to Earth. I never even heard him shut the door, but he's standing right behind me, waiting for me to finish my survey of the room.

I step further inside, until I'm next to the leather-covered spanking bench in its middle.

Needing to feel its texture, I run my fingers along the smooth surface. An adjustable floor-mounted set of stocks stands next to it, and a St. Andrew's cross up against the far wall. A comfortable-looking leather couch is against the other wall.

Then I finally turn back to Keegan, unable to keep the smile off my face. "It's all I hoped and more. It's… I don't have the words. There's just something really… exciting about being in here."

"Any guilt, shame?"

I pause, thinking about it. "Not yet." I shake my head. "Not at all… yet. I'm too excited. That's a little weird, isn't it?"

"No. Well, maybe a little, but everyone's a little weird when you come down to it. My job isn't to make you less weird, it's to help you accept your particular brand of weirdness."

With a nod, I spin one more time to take in every-thing. I wet my lips and ask him, with a mix of trepidation and excitement, "So when do we start?"

He takes a step closer while he removes his suit jacket, throwing it aside onto the couch. "Call me Sir."

I look up at him, the way he looms over me and makes me feel small. And like I'm his. "Yes, Sir."

"Go stand in the middle of the room, facing away from me. You remember the safewords?"

"Yes, Sir," I reply while obeying his order.

"Repeat them to me."

"Red to stop, yellow to pause and discuss."

"Good. Legs apart, hands crossed behind your back, eyes straight ahead." His commands rattle off in quick order, and I stop in place, doing my best to obey. I can't quite decide whether to try to push away or embrace the tingling that's firing up in my gut. Sometimes the line between guilt and excitement is impossible to draw. To keep steady, I fix my gaze on the St. Andrew's cross.

Keegan approaches, following me across the play-room. His dress shoes clack clearly against the hard floor. He moves into my peripheral vision, but I don't dare glance in his direction.

He hasn't given me permission.

"Good." His voice is lower now, no longer conversational. It's harder, a voice for giving orders. A shiver crawls down my back, enticingly dangerous. With my hands clasped and my straight posture, I can't help but be aware of how my position presses my breasts out against my shirt.

Can't help wonder if he notices.

Do I want him to?

Of course I do. He's an attractive man, and there's something in the back of my mind screaming, "Yes!" But he's not supposed to. I know that much about how this works. And even if I wasn't his client, would he want to?

It's wrong, but I want to think he sees me as a woman. To know he's not just doing what he'd do for anyone with my issues. I'm going to need therapy for my therapy soon. This stuff is confusing.

He walks around behind me. "Submission isn't just about taking orders. If all you're doing is taking orders, you're working a job. It's about giving up a part of yourself, if only for a short while, to let me into your mental space. Do you think you could do that?"

"I…" I trail off, not sure about the answer. Could I? My mind spins.

I should never give up any part of myself.

I want to give myself up.

Submitting is shameful. It makes me vulnerable.

But I want to be vulnerable. At least sometimes.

Give them an inch, and they'll take all of you.

I dream of being taken.

And then wake up feeling guilty for dreaming about it. How much worse would it be if I actually let it happen?

But how much better than my dream might the reality be?

I'm trapped in a loop of desire and denial that I don't know how to escape from, but dammit, I can try.

Drawing a deep breath, I reply with all the confidence I can muster, "Yes." And I believe it, despite every little misgiving that's niggling at me. "At least to you. I trust you."

There's a bit of a pause before he responds. "Good. Thank you."

"Sure thing," drops out of me before I can stop it. Doesn't seem very appropriate for what we're doing, but there was a bit of dead space and I needed to fill it.

He chuckles softly. "Are you ready for more, then? To take it to the next level?"

I nod, though goosebumps are rising up my arms and the little hairs at the back of my neck stand up. What does he mean by next level?

"I'm not going to actually tie your wrists, but I want you to imagine that I have and keep them behind you and together at all times. Can you do that?" He moves behind me and puts his hands on my wrists. His grip feels more inescapable than any handcuffs ever would.

"Yes," I nearly whisper.

"Yes what?"

"Yes… Sir." I have to go deeper than I expect to force out the "Sir". Earlier, I'd been playful. I could play it off with a kind of nonchalance. But here, in the dark room with him in a suit and me exposed in the middle of it all, shit just got real.

11

MIRANDA

H e pulls my wrists back and crosses them. "Leave them there."

"Yes, Sir."

He lets go, gently, like you'd release a rescue animal into the wild, but I keep my wrists where I promised. He pats my upper arm gently. "Good. When I'm in command, you will attend to me. Pay attention. Until I say we're done, or you call your safeword, you're mine."

Mine.

I was okay until he said that. Now, suddenly I'm overwhelmed by a heat that fills me, all the way down. Closing my eyes, I let the word fill me with its implications, with its force. Mine. It's so forbidden, and yet, right now, it feels so incredibly right. Any thoughts of guilt and shame flitter away as if all the butterflies in my stomach just escaped.

"Yes, Sir." This time, the words come out with more confidence.

"I'm going to command you into some new positions. These will challenge you more than the last time. Remember your safewords."

"Yes, Sir."

He points at the spanking bench. "Climb on board." When I hesitate, he steps closer. "Safeword if you need it. There's no shame in it."

I shake my head. I can do this. I approach it, trying to figure out how to get on.

"Knees here." He points. "Rest your stomach across here, and your face here. I'll adjust it to fit you comfortably once you're up."

I look at the bench, then at him, then back at the bench, keeping my hands crossed behind me the whole time. Even if the bondage isn't real, in my mind my wrists are inextricably connected. He's keeping me helpless, so I have to depend on him.

It feels like a test, to see if I am able to give him that control too. For now at least, I am. "Sir, I can't get up on my own."

"That's fine." There's a new rasp in his voice, a huskiness I don't remember hearing before. As if his voice wasn't sexy enough already. "I'll steady you. Right leg up here, good..." With his help, I'm soon in position. He presses a button and the pads under my legs move up just a little, then he looks me over. "Does that feel okay? Tell me if you're uncomfortable."

I test my position, but it's solid. I feel safe, at least from falling. "It's good, Sir."

"Excellent. You're doing very well."

I reply much more calmly than I feel, "Thank you, Sir."

He takes a step back, but stays in my field of view. He's looking me over, his expression serious. It feels like he's making sure I'm positioned properly, and it does make me feel safer. A little. Also really exposed. The way I'm positioned, my butt is up in the air, making it a bit of a target.

I swallow. He's not actually going to spank me, is he? A rush of conflicting feelings washes over me. I mean, I wouldn't want him to actually put his hands on me like that, would I? I shouldn't.

Bad girls get what they deserve. Oh God, where did that come from? Forcing the memory away, I press it deep into the recesses of my mind. I refuse to let Dad's legacy mess with me after so many years. Take deep breaths, focus on Keegan, focus on the bench, focus on anything that's not the past. Focus on the fact that a drop dead gorgeous dominant therapist with sex for a voice is about to give me a hands on lesson.

"Fuck, that's beautiful," Keegan whispers behind me. It's quiet enough that I don't know if he realizes that I heard. I might not have, had my senses not already been on high alert, but it brings me back into the moment. I'm here with Keegan, and I trust him.

"Thank you, Sir," I respond in almost as low a whisper. The room is so full of tension that it feels as if the slightest sound might break it.

He moves out of my field of vision. The temptation to look up to see what he's doing is strong, but he wouldn't approve. He hasn't said so explicitly, but I know it, and I don't want to do anything wrong—not out of fear, I realize, but because I don't want to disappoint him. Is this what submission is supposed to feel like?

He returns, his footsteps echoing in the small room. He comes around behind me, but when he stops, he's just at the edge of my vision. At the height my eyes are at, all I see is his legs in starkly creased black suit pants and, hanging next to them, a cluster of black leather strands. A flogger.

I bite my lip. There are a lot of bookmarks on my computer to different floggers, and videos of their use. They're the most beautiful whips, and the one he's got is a mix of black and deep purple tails. I can't stop looking at it.

"Has anyone ever whipped you?"

Wide-eyed, I shake my head as much as I can without losing contact with the bench.

"Speak when I ask you a question."

"No, Sir."

"I'll give you a chance to say no, without using safewords. If this is a hard no, then I'll put the flogger away and think of something else."

I'm not sure how he does it, but he makes me feel safe like no one else ever has, even when he's standing behind me with a whip. I trust him to do this. I want him to do this.

Clenching my fists behind my back, I draw a deep breath. Dad's already forgotten. "Go ahead, Sir."

He lets out a short breath of air, as if he'd been holding it while waiting for my answer. "Very good. I'll start easy. Remember your safewords."

"Yes, Sir." I clench my eyes shut and wait.

The only warning I get is a slight rush of air as he swings the flogger. A moment later, it connects with my ass, stinging even through my skirt and underwear. It aches, but not enough to really hurt. My skin tingles as blood rushes to the surface, and even when he pulls the flogger away, I can sense the red hot stripes the leather strips would surely leave behind if he was using more strength.

I can only imagine what that'd feel like if I were bare.

I have to admit I'd been a little unsure as to whether I would like this in practice, even as much as I've watched, read and heard about it. Can you really enjoy being in someone's power and let them punish you, just because they feel like it?

As my panties dampen and a surge tightens my stomach, I find myself pushing my ass back, eagerly awaiting the next strike.

So yes, apparently you can. I do, and it's amazing.

He swings again, a little lower this time, just above where my thighs meet my ass. One of the strips connects below the rest, smooth leather licking actual bare skin just below the hem of my skirt. I draw a short breath between clenched teeth, shocked more than hurt.

I want to take everything he can give.

My eyes are still shut, but in my mind, he's standing over me, broad and powerful with the flogger clenched in one hand, watching me react to his actions. He's in power, making me feel things whether I've asked for them or not.

Making me his.

"You're quiet."

"Yes, Sir," I force out.

"But you're okay?"

"Yes, Sir."

He strikes again, the soft leather hitting the fabric of my skirt, with a muffled thud. It would be a sharp crack against my bare skin, but what would it feel like if I wasn't wearing anything? An image of him standing over me bare-chested as he whips my exposed ass makes me shiver deeply.

The next hit is harder, the swish louder and the stinging trails of leather more obvious where they slide across me. I grunt and clench my jaw against the slowly building burn the flogger leaves behind, along with a tingle that worms its way straight to my core, super-heating it.

Another. My breathing comes faster, and my whole body vibrates with tension. All common sense would dictate that I should stop him, call out my safeword and get away from this kind of craziness. Mom would call this straight out abuse, forget about submission. There would already be police reports in the process of filing. But despite that, my excitement is unlike any I've ever felt before. Calling out any kind of safeword is the furthest from my mind as adrenaline courses through me, and my ass pushes back on its own in anticipation of the next blow.

The next one actually stings, the flogger landing across the backs of my thighs, right where the hem stops and my bare thighs begin. Not just a single strand across bare skin this time, but several. Oh crap.

"Yellow," I call out, and open my eyes.

"Are you okay?"

I find Keegan crouching right in front of me, so quick that it seems like he's teleported. I nod, still in position. "I don't have anything to cover my legs. Don't leave marks that will show when I leave."

Relief floods his eyes. Did he think I didn't like this? I just wish I'd thought to bring pants.

"I'll be careful. None of these marks will last much past the session, but I'll leave exposed skin alone." He pulls the strands of leather through his hand as he talks. I catch myself licking my lips as I watch. "Was that it?"

"Huh? Oh, yeah, that was it."

He grins. "Game on, then."

I bite my lower lip as I smile back. "Yes, Sir."

He stands, and I listen to each step with anticipation until he stands behind me. A second or two passes, and then the whip comes down with a swoosh and connects right on my ass. That was the hardest one yet, and I yelp. I get an urge to put my fist in my mouth so I won't make too much noise, but I'm supposed to pretend that I'm cuffed. This would be a lot easier if I actually were.

What I definitely don't do is use my safeword.

It's weird. This should freak me out, but all I'm feeling is a sort of catharsis. I've been thinking about this so long, and for the first time, I'm actually doing it. Not just getting spanked, though I've certainly had that fantasy more than once, but being in this situation, where I have no choice. I mean, I do, with safewords and all that, but also I don't. I'm at Keegan's mercy until he sees fit to let me up, and meanwhile, I'm free to enjoy being dirty and kinky, because it's not my choice anymore.

Until he's done, I'm his, and I love that.

We fall into a rhythm, and it actually takes several moments before I realize he's not flogging me anymore. Instead, the warmth of his finger touches my cheek, scooping up a tear I didn't know I shed and wiping it from my face.

"We're done."

I look up at him, my face still pressed against the seat. "We are, Sir?"

God, I want to look up at the smile he's giving me every day. A pang of guilt hits me the moment I think it, and it's not even over what we've just done. It's for expecting him to do anything beyond his job, or even imagining that he'd want to.

"We are." He holds a hand out. "You're not cuffed anymore. Come on."

I let him help me gingerly off the bench, and only then do I realize how unsteady I am. "I think I need to sit."

"Of course. Let me bring you to the couch." And with that, he picks me up. I'm not a tiny girl, but he's got me right up in his arms as if I weigh nothing. I knew he was built, but I had no idea how strong.

"Thank you, Sir."

He chuckles. "You don't have to call me that anymore." Then he turns and sinks into the couch with me still in his arms, so that when we land, I'm curled right up in his lap, leaning into his warmth.

Should we be this close? We're just in a professional relationship, right? Is this cuddle therapy? I could grow to like that.

"Given your apparent love of Google, I assume you're familiar with aftercare."

I nod, my face pressing into his chest so I can hear his heartbeat. "It always sounded nice."

"It's supposed to be." His powerful arms flex, pulling me closer. "After putting you through that, I thought it was only right that I try to give you the proper care as well. I hope you're okay with that. If I'm getting too close here or being inappropriate in any way, please stop me."

I cling harder. "Don't even think about it."

"How do you feel?" His one hand plays with my hair. I'm not sure he even realizes that he's doing it. This is a lot closer than I expected us to get today. Maybe ever.

I don't know how to feel about it. Is it real? Or is this just part of the exposure therapy? Right now, as I think about what we just did, it really seems like we've stepped over a line somewhere along the way. But therapy comes in many different forms, apparently. Is it a line I'm comfortable with having overstepped?

That's the big question. And how does Keegan see it? If I feel like this is something more, and he just thinks of it as part of his job, well, how freaking awkward is that?

But right now, he's asking about my guilt complex. I think so, anyway, so pushing away thoughts about how much what we just did means or doesn't mean, I look for those feelings instead.

"Guilty, you mean? Not yet. I'm too content right now."

He hmms, nodding slowly. "I think that's a good sign."

"I mean, I know it's coming. Sometimes it's kind of like… like walking down an alley. Everything's okay, but at the end of it there's a shadow and you know it means someone's waiting right around the corner to jump you, even if you can't see them yet."

"At the risk of stretching the analogy too far, can't you turn around and walk in the other direction?" There's no judgement in the question. Exploration maybe.

I shake my head, stroking my cheek against his broad chest in the process. "No. It's one of those alleys where someone's furiously bricking it up behind you as you go. The only way is forward."

"Right, one of those alleys," he replies as if they're a real thing and as common as streetlights.

"There might be a people mover floor too, like they have at the airports."

"This alley seems really set on getting you to the end."

My lips twitch. "Yeah, it's a really stupid alley."

We sit quietly for a while. His fingers still toy with my hair, but I don't mind. It's reassuring.

Comfortable. My hour must be over by now, right? I turn up to talk to him.

"Hey, isn't—"

"Listen, we—"

Just as I look up, he looks down, and suddenly we're face to face, only an inch or so between the tips of our noses. His deep emerald eyes bore into mine, and all we see is the other. His arm wrapped around my waist to keep me in place tightens, the fingertips of his open hand pushing into my back.

"We—"

"I—"

He licks his lips, and my eyes follow the path of his tongue intently as it moves. I swallow once, then whisper, "I'm sorry, Sir."

"Wha—"

And that's all he gets out before I press my lips to his. He stiffens for a moment, but then his grip on me tightens even further, pulling me closer. Reaching up, I wrap my arms around his powerful neck, and cling to him as we lose ourselves in each other.

His kiss is as good as he looks, which is saying something. He works magic with his tongue, chasing mine around while we cling to each other like we'd float away forever if we let go. Shivers race up and down my skin, leaving tingling trails in their wake. I've never felt as safe in my life as I do in his arms.

When we finally separate, it's reluctantly, coming to the surface like we're emerging from underwater. We both draw deep breaths and face each other. His expression is difficult to read, but there's an intensity in his eyes that's impossible to look away from.

Even so, he pushes me gently until there's a little distance between us, even though I'm still curled up in his lap.

I screwed up. "Oh, I'm so sorry. I shouldn't have — I mean, you must think that—"

"No, I'm the one who should apologize. I should've stopped you, not—" He sighs. "This was a very intense session. Emotions run high, and it can make us—us, not just you—do things that aren't appropriate. I'm really sorry. If you want to file a complaint—"

"A what? No! But—"

"Exposure therapy might have been a bad idea. You're reacting too strongly to me, and… fuck, I'll admit it. I'm having a hard time maintaining a separation between the personal and the professional."

I lick my lips nervously. "What if I don't mind it getting personal?"

"It can't get personal. It's unethical." His expression is pained, as if even uttering those words hurts him.

I know he's right. Of course he's right. But what also feels right?

This.

Him over me, me in his arms, us together. If I could undo our professional relationship, so we could just start over, I'd do it in a heartbeat, but that's not how this works. And if we only met personally, would I have ever dared to open up to him like this?

Not likely.

"So now what, then? I want you as my therapist. You're the only one who's managed to get me to… do this." I gesture around us. "You've helped me dare things I thought I never would."

"And I want to help you."

"What if I fire you?"

"What?"

"If you're no longer my therapist, then it's not a problem, right?"

He sighs, though there's a hint of a smile tugging at his lips. "It doesn't work like that. All it will look like is that I groomed you to be my submissive. And you need to consider that it might be true. Not intentionally, but I'm in a position of power over you."

"I like having you in power over me." It just slips out of me, but it's true.

A short laugh escapes him, even with the gravity of our situation. "That might be the problem. You need to consider if what you're feeling for me is real, or if you're just forming an attachment to the first person you feel safe with." Seriousness returns to his expression. "Listen, I want to see you succeed with this."

Oh no. "Don't say you're dropping me. Don't you dare."

He shakes his head. "I'm not. I have to have enough confidence in my abilities to do this right, but we're going to have to back off a little. I will work on you, but I think taking you here was going too far. We'll have our next session back at the office."

I nod, my mind racing with what-ifs. Trying to find a way to deny what he's saying but coming up with nothing. It's not the end of the world. I'll still see him. "Okay. I'll call in the morning to schedule it."

He reaches out as if to stroke my hair, but stops halfway and pulls back. "That sounds good. I suppose we should get out of here."

What would he do if I just threw myself over him? Push me away and recommend a new therapist probably. Even if it worked out the way I hoped, what would it solve? He'd come to his senses afterwards. Besides, maybe he's right and I just need a little time to cool down. I'm not sure he realizes exactly how worked up he's gotten me.

A few minutes later, after he's walked me to my car, the thrum of the music inside the club is a muted backdrop as a cool wind blows down the street, getting up under my skirt. I shiver. We're facing each other, and my first instinct is to hug him goodbye. I reach up just as he puts his hand out for a shake.

Crap. Distance, right.

So we both switch, making this even more awkward, him raising both hands and me lowering mine for a shake. He laughs while I blush, then takes my hand before I can embarrass myself again, but instead of shaking, he just holds it. "We'll talk soon."

"Yes. Definitely."

He watches until I'm driving away, waving one last time in my rear view mirror. I finally find someone who manages to tick all my boxes, and it's just my luck that he's about the only man on the planet I can't have. I touch my fingers to my lips. That kiss will be with me for a long time, even if it's the only one we get.

12

MIRANDA

Before I enter my apartment, I slide my hands over the backs of my thighs. The skin is spotless, but I can still feel tingles, deep inside, from Keegan's flogger. I almost wish there were marks, but of course that would raise a lot of questions I really don't feel like answering for my mother.

God, I can't believe he kissed me! That I kissed him. And the flogging. That was amazing. I overcame my fear. And for once, I feel proud, still vibrating from the adrenaline rush, even now.

Fuck you, Dad.

I don't carry the same anger towards Mom, because she's as scarred as I am. Probably more.

But even still, now I somehow have to hide my elation at what I've just dared to do, or dared to let him do, from her.

Why can't we both live in a world where I can be into a man who can both be a gentleman when it counts and who will happily flog my ass when I want him to?

As I close the door behind me, Mom calls from the living room. "You're home. Where were you so late? I was getting ready to call someone."

"I told you I'd be out a little late tonight, remember? I figured the knitting fair would keep you busy anyway."

"Not too busy for my girl. Besides, how late did you think it would go? It was interesting, though. I picked up a few new patterns, so be prepared for something fresh for this year's Christmas sweater." Mom's already smiling in my direction as I come into the living room. She looks me up and down, then narrows her eyes suspiciously. "Well, look at you. Were you on a date or something?"

"Of course not! So, what else did you do today?" I deflect, frantically searching for a story that might explain why I would be dressed up for my job at a coffee shop.

Her suspicion doesn't go away, but she accepts my derail, at least for now. "Well, I mostly walked around for a while after I blew my yarn budget. You know how those things are, I have to be strict with myself or I'd end up with a second mortgage." She laughs. "Still, it was fun to explore. There was a lot more variety than the Craft Mart carries back home, let me tell you."

"See? There are benefits to living in a city."

"Oh sure, though I'd feel a lot safer with you out of it. Is it really so much better here? You've been away for a long time. Is it so terrible to come home for a visit? I miss you."

"What? No! You know I love you, Ma."

She smiles. "I know. And I love you too. But you don't exactly call or write very often. Gladys and Debbie miss you too, and it'd be nice to see you in our church group again."

I try to match her smile but it's hard. Her group is a strange blend of warning me away from temptation on the one hand and, as if these things happen in parallel universes, trying to find a nice man to set me up with on the other. They're nice people at heart, but well, there's a reason I moved.

"Well, you know, I'm busy. Learning the new job. Spending time with friends. Keeping out of trouble." Watching people get spanked and whipped and dripped with wax. Sometimes figged, but that's for special occasions. Obviously, I don't bring those bits up.

"You better be keeping out of trouble. In this town, you're like a lost little lamb surrounded by wolves."

I roll my eyes. "I like to think I've developed a bit more street smarts than that." Maybe Mom is the one who should find a good man, someone who can show her that they're not all manipulative, abusive assholes.

Like I have. My lips curve into a smile just thinking about Keegan.

"Are you telling me that no one ever hassles you? You're working in a cafe, and it makes me terrified. Working directly with strangers all day long. How am I supposed to believe that someone as beautiful as my only daughter isn't attracting all sorts of crazies?'"

I take a deep breath and try not to let her get me too riled up. "Believe it or not, my days aren't that bad. Not all men are predators."

"I never said they were," she says with a scowl.

"You didn't have to. It's pretty obvious what you think. Look, the worst I get is people who think being polite is for losers, and even if someone did cause trouble, my boss is right there. Aaron's like six foot five and almost as wide. Trust me, nobody steps out of line with him around."

"You shouldn't have to be dependent on a *man* to keep you safe." The way she says man makes it clear she isn't convinced. "You can't trust them. You know that."

"I can't live in a bubble either, Mom. There are good guys too." I picture Keegan's dark green eyes and the way he was looking at me earlier. That was even sexier than the wild things he did.

"You're seeing someone, aren't you?" Mom sounds almost betrayed.

Yes? No?

I'm dying to talk about it, even if Mom is my only option at the moment.

But how much do I tell her? I mean, obviously, there are some things I definitely don't tell her. No way, no how. And does it matter? Keegan's already made it obvious that there can be no us. Still, I was never able to lie to Mom for long, so I'll sort of let the cat out of the bag. "There might be someone I'm interested in. Nothing official, though."

"Does he treat you with the respect you deserve?"

Does whipping me with a flogger count? I ask myself idly, knowing what mom's answer would be. "He treats me the way I'd like him to."

"What does he do?"

Oh God, there's another avenue I don't want to go down. Why did I open my big mouth? Then again, Mom wouldn't have let it go if I'd said no. "He's a doctor."

There's a pause. "I don't trust men with power."

I sit down next to her on the couch with a sigh, putting my arm around her. "I know you don't. I was there too, you remember? Dad was… a sadistic asshole."

"Language!"

"Are you going to tell me he wasn't?" I squeeze her harder. Neither of us likes talking about those days, but they come up often when we do talk. Too often. Just another reason I'm not a huge fan of going home.

You'd better behave, or I'll show you that bad girls get what they deserve! Dad's voice comes unbidden into my head.

God, what's with me lately? Maybe it's the therapy. In order to get better, some nasty scabs are getting torn off. Ugly memories floating to the surface. I remember the last time he said that very clearly now that it's in my head. Right before we ran away. Right before he finally showed me. With his fists. I shudder and glance at Mom. She's looking away, so hopefully she didn't notice.

Her mouth is a thin, straight line when she does look at me. "No. He was. Still is, for all I know. But I don't want to hear that kind of language out of you, young lady. It's another reason I don't think this city living is good for you." Her expression softens. "Anyway, just because this man you're seeing is a doctor doesn't mean that he's safe. Your father was a CEO, you know. For all the things he lacked, money wasn't one of them."

I nod. And when we ran off, obviously we didn't get a cent of it, because he could afford expensive lawyers and we couldn't. There was never enough proof to get him nailed down for anything. In the law's eyes, it was her word against his. Mom gave up quickly, too worried that he'd insist on shared or even full custody just to spite her if she pushed for child support. We were just happy to be safe.

"I'd like to meet him before I leave."

"Dad?"

"What? No! This *unofficial* man of yours."

"Oh, Keegan." As soon as the name is out of my mouth I know I made a mistake.

"Is that his name? What is that? Irish?"

Crap. "You know, I have no idea, but he's very busy with his patients. I can try, but I can't guarantee anything."

"If he respects you, he'll come to meet your mother," she says firmly, like there really is no other option.

What have I done? Given how we parted earlier tonight, I'll be lucky if he'll willing to see me in public outside his office, much less come visit me at home. But once mom latches onto something, she's like a bulldog. "I'll try calling him after dinner."

"Why don't you call him now?"

Jeez. "Because I'm hungry." And need a little time to think. "What do you want to eat?"

She frowns at being overruled, but she nods. "What are the options?"

"Spaghetti, unless you want to go to the store. I didn't get a chance to shop."

"No, that's fine. So tell me about this Keegan. What do you do together? Where is he from? How long have you known him?"

While I rummage through my cabinets for sauce, I speak over my shoulder, "That's a lot of questions."

"Mmhm," is all she replies as she takes a seat on one of the stools on the other side of the island that separates my kitchen from the living room. She's obviously not letting me off the hook.

So what do I tell her? If I give her his full name, even someone as technologically backward as my mother would know how to use Google and I'm not sure the things she'd find would exactly set her mind at ease. I don't know where he's from, though he sounds kind of north east. And I really don't like lying, especially to Mom. She's got this sixth sense for picking out when I'm fibbing. I'm already skirting dangerously close to the edge.

"Our relationship is pretty new, so I don't know that much of his background yet, but we talk a lot so I'm sure I can fill you in later if this whole thing comes to anything. We're not really *together* together. I like him, but no one's committed to anything, you know?"

"You're being evasive. Don't think you can fool me, sweetie. I can see it in your eyes. You look like I did back when..." She trails off.

I sigh. "Fine, give me a minute." I set a pot of water to boil and shake out the spaghetti. "Let me see if he's free tomorrow, but he works late so I can't make any promises." Maybe he'll have some idea on how we can handle this. God knows I could use some ideas. "Keep an eye on the water?"

"Sure." She comes around while I grab my phone off the coffee table and unlock it. I quickly tap out a short email, since I still don't have his private number.

Hey. Mom is convinced you're my new boyfriend and she wants to meet you. Please save me!

I do some quick Googling of his name in the meantime, as much to see how much trouble I'd be in if Mom somehow got it into her head to do it, as to see what else I can learn about him. Mom's stirring the spaghetti into the water, so I have a few minutes.

Crap, there's a lot. Papers submitted in college, his doctorate thesis on the cathartic effects of corporal punishment in a consensual setting, obviously his professional website, and even some high school pictures. There really is nothing private anymore, is there?

I'm saving a few pictures for later perusal when my mail plings.

Did you try telling her that we're not dating? Why does she even think we're together? We talked about this at the session.

He's right, of course. I've already messed up by letting her think it. Maybe I can convince her that she's wrong after all. "Mom, about that guy…"

"Yes? When is he coming?"

"I was fibbing, okay? There really isn't a guy. I just wanted you to understand that I'm feeling pretty attached to living here, and I wasn't sure how to make you realize it. I'm sorry."

There's a short pause. "Nice try, but now I definitely have to meet him. I don't know why you're trying to hide him from me, and I'm getting worried. If he's bad news, I can't let you stay here."

I'm not sure what she could do to take me away, but I really don't want that kind of conflict with Mom, so I take the path of least resistance. "Fine. I'll see what I can do." I tap out a response to Keegan.

She's like a badger once she gets an idea in her head. I know it's dumb, but I might've let it slip that I was interested in someone and she ran with it. Please? If only to keep her off my back?

The reply isn't long in coming.

You want me pretend to be your boyfriend? There are so many good reasons why that's a bad idea. Isn't there someone else who could do this, if you absolutely have to do it?

I can hear his frustration in my head even if I'm just reading the words. He's right, of course. I could ask my boss, but he'd never let me live it down, and I'm sure Amber could find me someone, but she'd be even worse.

Besides, they wouldn't be Keegan.

Listen, I know this breaks with everything you said, but there's no one else I feel comfortable asking. Please. Just come here, talk to her a bit and we can leave together. You can just drop me off at a cafe or something, and I'll just read for a while and then head home. Whatever, as long as you seem nice and she gets off my back. She's not going to let this go, and she's terrified I'm being secretive because something's wrong.

I feel so dumb writing it, but I send it anyway. This is the kind of stupid ploy teenage me might have thought of if she hadn't been so stupidly well behaved.

It takes long enough before the next message comes that I start to doubt my last one got through. Either that, or it did and he's trying to decide if he should report me to someone for harassment, but then my phone dings again.

Fine. It's against my better judgment, and you can expect this to come up in our next session. Does tomorrow after work sound good? I'll come pick you up at 6pm, and be on my best behavior.

Oh, thank God.

Thank you, thank you, thank you. I've told her you're a doctor, but if you can leave the therapist bit out of it, that'd be great. Obviously nothing about kink, but I don't see exactly how that'd come up anyway. Other than that, I've told her it's a pretty new thing, and I don't know too much about your background yet.

"So, is your doctor friend too busy for your mother?"

I jump, so absorbed in the messages that she scares the hell out of me by plopping two steaming bowls of spaghetti on the coffee table in front of me. I very deliberately turn so my screen faces away from her.

"We're just figuring out the details. Thanks for the food."

She smiles. "Just make yourself at home. Mi casa es su casa."

"Right. Thanks."

Relax, I'm sure it'll go fine. It's like a good scene: communication is key, both what we say and what we don't say.

Easy for him to say.

Thanks for the lesson, BDSM swami. Have to go.

Quickly signing off the email, I tack on my cell number. Even as I'm getting up from the couch, my phone trills, notifying me of a new text. I check it immediately.

This doesn't change anything.

His reminder that we shouldn't be together deflates a little of my relieved mood, but at least

I'm not feeling any of the usual shame or guilt right now. Probably too stressed.

"Did I ever mention how proud I am of you?" Mom says with a loving smile.

Oh no, wait, there it is.

13

MIRANDA

K eegan's, right on time, pulling up in front of my apartment in a black sedan. I'm not really a car girl, but it looks nice. I watch him from behind the curtains in my living room window, trying not to drool on them at the sight of him. He's either wearing the same suit he took me to the club in, or one much like it. I'm glad I thought to put on makeup and a pretty outfit, even if this is all pretend.

Mom gives me a skeptical look. "Are you sure about this man? You don't seem to really know him very well."

I sigh. "Relax. We'll be in public the whole time. Besides, you were the one who wanted me to set this up."

She snorts. "I want you to move home where I can keep a better eye on you."

I let it lie, mostly because the doorbell rings. "Shh. He's here. Be nice." I try to sound more confident than I feel.

It's funny. If Mom wasn't here, I'd probably have a lot of the same reservations she does. God knows my father's behavior did me no favors, and Mom and her church group only rubbed it in. Tack onto that my hint of anxiety, and well... yeah. But now that I have to defend him from Mom, I don't have time to think about that.

I open the door.

It's only been a day since I've seen him, but having him up close still takes my breath away. The suit fit him perfectly, tight over the chest and shoulders and crisply ironed, showing off his distinctive V shape that I love so much. His pants are just a little tight across the fronts of his powerful legs, with crisp creases.

His hair is neat without a hair out of place and in his left hand are two bouquets of flowers. His gorgeous green eyes have an amused glint in them.

I'm speechless. What's more surprising is the heavy sigh next to me. Really? If not even Mom is immune, I might stand a chance yet.

He holds out his hand to Mom while glancing bemusedly between the two of us. "Hello. I'm Keegan York. You must be Miranda's sister."

Oh God. That was cheesy. Pretty sure that's not the way to get Mom's approval.

He smiles, and I get a little weak in the knees.

"Mother," Mom stutters out as she takes his hand. "I'm Miranda's mother."

I blink. What planet is this on? Is my weakness for Keegan genetic?

"Of course. My mistake," he manages to respond without a trace of irony. "I'm very pleased to meet you. You've raised a strong and self-reliant woman."

He managed to say just about the perfect words to get on Mom's good side. I guess he earned that degree in psychology. The effect on Mom is immediate. Even if she weren't already struck by his good looks—which is still unbelievable to me—the pleased expression on her face is like the sun just rose in the room.

"Thank you." She smiles broadly. "I've done my best. It's so refreshing to meet a man who actually notices that, rather than just how pretty she is."

"Well, I hope I don't offend when I say that she's that too."

"No, of course not." Her eyes flutter. Mom's freaking eyes, fluttering. I swear, I just opened the front door and fell into another dimension.

"I brought some flowers. I hope that's all right." He holds a bouquet out to each of us. Roses. Mine are red and pink, while Mom's are yellow and orange.

I don't care what Mom thinks of the dangers of men who come courting you. I take my flowers happily, pressing them against my face to inhale their sweet scent. "Thank you. They're beautiful." His answering smile makes me want to kiss him, but I can't quite bring myself to do it in front of Mom, especially after how our last kiss turned out.

Mom accepts her bouquet and smells it, just like I did. Really? Is a hot enough guy all it takes for Mom to forget her paranoia? Then again, I suppose she didn't always feel the way she does. She ended up with me, didn't she?

When she lowers the flowers from her face, she beams at Keegan. "They're very nice, thank you. Are you two in a hurry? I'd love to chat a little."

Keegan checks his wrist quickly, his watch looking very big and expensive. "Sure, we've got a few minutes. Maybe another day we can find some time for a proper sit-down."

"Wonderful. I feel I should be asking your intentions with my daughter, but you'll only give me the answer you want me to hear. So, we'll do a speed round. Where are you from? How did you meet my daughter? Where do you see this going?"

Oh my God. "Mom! Lay off the third degree, could you?"

"I'm your mother, sweetie. I have every right to learn a little bit about the man you've chosen to let into your life."

"Mom…"

Keegan puts up a hand. "No no, it's fine. I don't mind. I'm from a bunch of places, really. My parents are from New Hampshire, but we moved to Arizona when I was pretty young. Then Mom got fed up with the heat, and we headed north to Washington, where I completed high school. I did my studies at different colleges until I finally got my doctorate at University of Michigan. Then, after a couple of years of internships and further studies, I came here and started my own practice."

Mom nods. "Impressive. I do love the Pacific Northwest, even if it rains all the time."

He reaches out and takes my hand. He's so warm, and yet I'm trembling. It's the first time we've done any actual public display of affection, and I'm not prepared for that. It's… really nice. It doesn't even feel like he's pretending.

"So… about how we met." He looks at me, and I cut a terrified glance right back at him.

"Uh, yes… that."

We really should've prepared a story for this, at least. It's the most obvious question. Keegan clears his throat. "It was at Wegman's actually. In the produce section."

"Oh yeah," I chime in. "He was shopping for melons, and—" I stop short. That sounded idiotic, and like a terrible innuendo, all at once.

His smile widens, but he just keeps running with it. "It's been a great season for them, especially the locally sourced ones. Amazing."

Seriously? He's going there?

Mom looks like she's trying to figure out if we're making fun of her or not. "Melons?" There's a distinctly skeptical tone to her voice.

"I know, it sounds ridiculous, but the cantaloupes were amazing that day."

"Cantaloupes," Mom parrots. Not even a question this time, just a disbelieving statement.

I have to save this before it goes out of control. "Yeah, we bumped into each other reaching for the same one, and it was a whole Lady and the

Tramp moment." I shrug. "We got to talking, and then talked some more, and then he bought me a hot chocolate at the cafe."

"Your daughter has quite the sweet tooth."

Mom nods. "She's always had a weakness for treats."

Since Keegan's hand is still holding mine, I use my other one to pull up his sleeve so I can see the face of his watch. "Hey, shouldn't we get going? We wouldn't want to miss our reservation."

"Oh, you're right, we should. Ms. Larson, it was a joy to meet you. Hopefully next time we'll have a little more time to chat." He crooks his arm for me to grab onto, and I happily link mine with his.

He gestures at the hallway. "Shall we?"

Amazingly, Mom doesn't make a single snide comment. Keegan works some serious magic.

"You two have fun tonight." Her eyes narrow as she looks right at him. "But not too much. I'm trusting you to keep my baby safe." I guess she needs to get in at least one barb.

Keegan smiles. "Safety is of the utmost importance to me, I assure you." I half expect him to
quote the safe, sane and consensual adage from all
the BDSM blogs.

"Then have a good time. I'll just curl up with a
book and relax here tonight. Don't worry
about me."

To be honest, by this point, I'm not. I'm too busy
pretending to go out with a hunky dominant
who's shown me that I can take a whipping
without losing my mind. It's all good, I just wish it
were real.

As soon as the door closes behind us, I look up at
him, and he looks down. Keegan's perfect
gentleman mask is gone in a flash, replaced by a
hungry look that slides slowly down from my face,
across my cleavage and then over my entire shape
to my toes before returning back up to gaze at me
with smoldering emerald heat in his eyes. For a
moment I wonder if he's reconsidered keeping
our relationship strictly professional.

It makes me want to climb him right there and
beg him to take me.

Hard.

But he softens his expression to something more neutral, and says quietly, "We should get going, before your mother gets suspicious." He's probably guessed that mom might be listening at the door. Keegan's totally got her pegged.

I need to find a way to lure feral Keegan back out. I give his arm a little squeeze, then tell him, "Lead on, Mr. Driver."

His car has a really smooth ride, and he drives with confidence. It's not long before he pulls up in front of an Italian place called Giuseppe's. "I took the liberty of reserving a table for us. Hope this is good."

"Wait, you're taking me to an actual date? What's going on here?" I look at him, flabbergasted. "Aren't you the one who said we needed more distance."

He shrugs, looking a little uncomfortable. "I didn't like the idea of just dropping you off somewhere on your own, and I don't know about you, but I need to eat dinner. Since your mother expects you to be out for several hours, and you were saying that while she's here, it'll be more difficult for you to make it to our sessions, I figured we could kill two birds with one stone."

I grimace. Spending more time with Keegan sounds great, but a session at a restaurant? That's not exactly romantic. "Really? What can we do there?" Does this mean he likes me after all? Or is he just being thoughtful? I don't know what to think.

He sends me a sly grin. "Oh, I have some ideas if you're game. But we can also talk. It's a casual atmosphere out in the open. So long as we're in public, I don't think we can get in too much trouble."

My stomach rumbles, making the decision for me. "Is this a bad time to mention I had spaghetti yesterday?"

"Oh." His face falls. "I can find another place if—"

"No!" I laugh. "Italian is fine. Honest. I'm starving."

"Good." He parks and gets out quickly enough to open my door before I've got myself together. "You look gorgeous tonight," he says as I step out.

"You're looking pretty good yourself, Sir," I counter playfully, then laugh at the brief flash in his eyes. He might find it unethical to pursue this connection we obviously have, but we've done too much for me to believe that he's not at all interested. That kiss we shared... I've never felt anything like it. Maybe he'll be on his best behavior, but I feel safe when I'm with him, and that means there's no reason I have to behave too.

The restaurant is cozy, and while we're not way overdressed, it straddles that divide between casual and formal. I cling to Keegan's arm. He'd look good anywhere, wearing anything. The greeter guides us to a table by a window that looks out onto the street. Outside, traffic streams by busily, but inside it's quiet and calm. It's the kind of place you can dress up for, but also relax in without it seeming stuffy.

I smile up at Keegan, and he rewards me with a brilliant smile of his own. Now that we're here and sitting across from each other I'm suddenly unsure as to what to say, so I blurt out the first thing that comes to mind. "I can't believe you had Mom wrapped around your finger like that. Normally, she'd be chasing you out at the end of a broom for being a threat to her precious daughter."

He laughs, then replies in a smooth voice, "Maybe she can tell I have your best interests at heart. I really do, Miranda."

My heart flops at the sincerity in his eyes. Oh jeez. Like I wasn't already falling hard enough for him. "If that were true, we could take this dinner back to your place," I mutter under my breath.

He stiffens again. "I should watch what I say. Despite how this might look, I didn't intend to imply anything by having dinner tonight. You know that, right?"

It looks like he's trying to convince himself as much as he is me. I can appreciate that. He's being strong. I like that about him, but while he wants to do what's right, in my opinion the right thing to do is me.

I let out a little sigh. I'm being unfair. He really is trying, and just because I'm feeling like a big ball of hormones doesn't mean that I have any right to jeopardize his career. On the other hand, it's not exactly easy to control how I feel.

A waitress comes by, classically Italian with long, lustrous brown hair and big brown eyes that latch right onto Keegan. I don't think she realizes, but she licks her lips while she waits for his order. I can't say I'm not a little jealous, but he hardly seems to notice her. He looks at me instead. "Do you like calamari?"

Do I ever. "Yes, please. That sounds delicious."

"I'd like an order to share, please," he says to her. "Other than that I think we'll need a little time."

"Sure thing," she nearly sighs before going to put in our order. Her hips swing enticingly with her steps, but Keegan looks only at me, and that pleases me to no end.

"So…" He leans forward, keeping his sexy voice low. I lean in too, so I can hear better. "I was thinking about the exposure therapy, and how it seems to get us into trouble when we're in private."

I nod eagerly, totally up for going somewhere private and getting into trouble. Down, girl. I'm just going to frustrate myself when I know it's not going to happen.

"Instead, we'll do it in public. Exposure, but no trouble."

My mind flits from one possibility to the next, from being ordered into weird positions to being flogged over my chair right here in the restaurant. There's something so illicit about my thoughts that I squirm a little in my seat, but he can't possibly be thinking of the types of things I am. "We'd get arrested," I whisper.

He chuckles at my shock. "As much as the idea of you in handcuffs is now going to distract me for the rest of the evening, that's not what I'm planning." He glances around, making sure no one's listening in. "I'm going to find ways to command you throughout the whole evening, right here where everyone can see."

My eyes widen. "You're crazy." A million feelings rush over me at once, knotting together as a solid clump in my gut. Fear, excitement, embarrassment, shame... just a little of everything. What can he make me do in a place full of people?

He watches me intently, waiting for a response. I can turn him down, and I'm sure he'd accept my no, but if this is the only way he's willing to play, can do I really want to? It's a trust fall, and so long as he's there to catch me...

I meet his gaze, determined and trying to look as confident as I want to feel. When I nod, a smile spreads on his face, sexy and tingles-down-below-inducing. I swallow once, nervously.

Suddenly, he's very much in charge.

"Take your panties off," he orders, voice low.

"What?" I squeak loudly in response. The couple at the next table over turn to look at me. I flash them a quick, hopefully reassuring, smile before turning back to him. "What?" I repeat in a lower voice. "Here?"

"Up to you, but I want them off before the appetizer is here."

He's insane. In public? This feels like a bigger step than the flogging. When I was alone with him, there was the safety of it only being the two of us. Now? If I twirl too fast, anyone might see.

I blink at him, eyes wide. "Is this supposed to be part of your exposure therapy? Because I don't think that's what they mean by exposure."

He laughs, eyes sparkling. "It's important for you to test your limits. How much trouble this gets us in is up to you."

"Easy for you to say. You won't be the one flying free." I hiss, but he's probably right. It's not like I'm wearing a miniskirt. I just have to stay mindful of how I move.

He points at a waiter coming this way with a tray. "That looks like our calamari."

Crap. Decision time. "Ok, but I'm going to use the restroom to do it."

"That's fine." He grins and leans back in his chair.

"I'll be right back."

"Just back there and to the left," he says and points.

"Thanks," I respond with a grimace.

I can't believe that I'm doing this, but I also can't deny that my heart's pounding like a jackhammer from the excitement. He might be right when he claims this is less intimate than a one on one session in a private room, but if he thinks this isn't trouble, he's so so wrong.

Two minutes later, I walk back to our table with a pink thong balled up in my trembling hand.

Is it a little breezy in here, or is that just me?

14

KEEGAN

When Miranda returns from the restroom, she looks so nervous that there's no doubt she obeyed. Am I going too far? I'm letting my own desire for her override my duties as her therapist, but I can't help it, and out here in the open, I can only go so far, right?

There's something in her hand, a quick flash of pink visible between her fingers. She looks at the table. "How's the calamari?

"Delicious." I pick a piece of deep fried squid off the plate and dip it in marinara sauce before slipping it into my mouth. They really are very good. "Would be even better with a little melon on the side."

She wrinkles her nose. "No thanks. And I'll have you know right now that we're not playing any games that end up with my cantaloupes on the table."

I laugh. She might be nervous, but her snappy comebacks are still there.

Miranda doesn't go straight to her seat. Instead, she bends in front of me. "You spilled a little sauce on your jacket. Here." She picks up my napkin from the table. And then, expertly enough that I should ask her later if she has any pickpocketing experience, she uses it to pretend dab at my jacket near the pocket while slipping a pink bundle into it with her other hand. "There, got it." She returns my napkin to the table with a mischievous smirk.

Well, there's frilly pink proof in my pocket. In my mind, I imagine the slide of the soft fabric of her skirt directly against her smooth skin and how she must be feeling every draft that comes by with a bit of trepidation. How she now has to be even more careful of how she moves. "Thank you. Well done."

Her lips spread into a grin that's part excitement and part relief, then she sits down and dabs her mouth with a napkin. From the way her eyes sparkle, their corners crinkling, I suspect there's one hell of a smile behind that innocent piece of cloth.

"So was it true? All that stuff you told Mom?" She wiggles a bit in her seat, probably getting used to going commando in a nice restaurant.

"About where I grew up and all that? Of course. I didn't see any reason to make anything up when I didn't have to. Why, was it adequate?"

"If I hadn't seen it myself, I'd never have believed how well she took to you. You have a way around the women of the Larson family, I'll say that much."

"I think one is more than enough for me to handle. If she's looking for a therapist, I'm sure I can field some recommendations."

Miranda pinches her lips. "She certainly could do with one. You've helped me a lot, you know. Even if you don't think we're right together, you've done more for my confidence in the last few weeks than years of pining have done for me. You're the kind of miracle worker I want all to myself."

Not right together.

The words sting. Because, fuck, if we weren't stuck in this situation, I could be all kinds of right for her. Beautiful, smart, sassy… and so damn responsive. Ordering her around gets my engine firing on all cylinders. I refuse to psychoanalyze myself right now, because I fear I already know what the diagnosis will be. I didn't have to take her out tonight, and I sure as hell didn't need to start playing games with her at the restaurant.

Am I enjoying the benefits of breaking a few boundaries? Sure. But mostly I just love the idea of her sitting across from me with nothing on underneath that beautiful dress. Forbidden fruit hanging right in front of my own face.

I school my expression to something I hope is professional. "I appreciate that. Thank you. I'm glad you feel this is working for you. You already seem so much more confident, so much stronger than you were that first day at my office."

We finish the appetizer over small talk, and our waitress is soon back with the main course. A tasty-looking ossobuco over risotto for me, but Miranda's seafood Alfredo looks good as hell too. And a big basket of focaccia rolls to go with it.

Miranda sighs and licks her lips. I picked well, it seems.

When our waitress comes back with a bottle of red wine, Miranda glances at me. "I couldn't drink the whole bottle myself. Aren't you driving?"

"I hadn't planned on drinking, but the food just calls for it. I'll call a cab when we're done and pick up the car tomorrow." After the waitress allows me to taste the wine, I nod, and she pours both of us glasses before leaving the bottle at our table.

"Why, thank you, good Sir." She stresses the Sir in a way that makes her meaning obvious. "You know, for this not being a real date, you're doing a pretty good impression." She smirks.

She's right, of course. Is this really therapy? Or just an exercise in frustration? I can't exactly claim I'm keeping a clinical distance here. "It's just another session. I've never liked being conventional in how I work, that's all."

Yeah, I'm not even fooling myself, much less her. The arched eyebrow I get in return over her glass as she takes another sip makes that clear.

Absentmindedly, I pat at my jacket pocket, making sure the little surprise I brought is still there. Something for her second assignment. She's right. I am crazy. Just for bringing that, if nothing else. But I'll keep telling myself it's for the therapy. Man is not a rational creature, but a rationalizing one.

"Are you ready for more?"

Her eyes widen, though it's not clear whether it's in excitement or apprehension. Maybe a little of both. "I guess so? I can't say I'm not a little scared."

I pull a handkerchief from my pocket and open it to reveal what I've kept hidden inside. It's a small plastic egg, pink and smooth. I hand it to her. "Put this in."

"What?" She eyes it curiously.

I glance around. "Quick, while no one's looking. Or are you trying to tell me that sitting around without panties on doesn't have you excited enough for it?"

"You're insane."

"And you're mine."

She shudders briefly at the words. Words I couldn't hold back. Not being able to get in trouble while in public was a bullshit idea. It only makes it that much more exciting. But it won't go too far. It can't. I have to get her home after this, and we're taking a cab. No opportunity, no trouble. And then I'll go home and let the fantasy of how things could've gone play through my dreams all night.

After a furtive look around, she quickly slips a hand under her skirt. Her eyes close briefly as she settles, and she returns her hand to the table, wiggling the fingers at me to show that she did it. There's just a hint of wetness glistening at the tips, and immediately I realize that I've put myself in a position where it wouldn't be wise for me to get up from the table for a while.

"I can't believe you brought something like that with you."

"All part of your therapy."

"Yeah, right." She wiggles a bit in her seat. "Your techniques are certainly creative."

"You have no idea." Slipping my hand into my jacket pocket, I slightly twist a knob on the little black remote I've got there. The expression on her face makes it very obvious at exactly which moment the vibration kicks in.

"Oh. It's—" She bites her lower lip and stares at me in shock. "Did you—"

I shrug. "Perhaps." I've barely turned it on. Enough vibration to be distracting, but no more. At least not yet.

Closing her eyes, she takes a deep breath and looks like she's trying to center herself. She whispers, "How long are you going to leave it on?"

"We'll see. Until it suits me to turn it off." I gesture at the table. "You should eat before your food gets cold."

"Easy for you to say," she grumbles.

I grin. "What was that? Turn it up, you said?" I reach for my pocket while looking her right in her terrified eyes.

"No, no, I'll eat. Thank you."

Picking up my knife and fork, I stab a piece of meat so tender it nearly falls right off the bone and cut it off. "You know, I should've known better than to order a saucy dish when I'm wearing a suit. You thought the spilled marinara was bad…" I pat my other pocket, the one with her panties in it.

A shiver runs through her, and she closes her eyes while breathing in through her cute nose. Something must've hit the right spot there for a moment. "You're so bad."

"Just you wait." I smile and try to eat without getting sauce all over my shirt.

15

MIRANDA

The vibration just doesn't stop. Constantly buzzing, low-key, but enough to keep me wiggling in my seat. It's not quite touching where I need it, so I keep trying to nudge the infuriating little egg to where it should be.

I'm pretty sure the food is delicious, but I barely taste it, I'm so focused on the sensations surging from between my legs. It's funny. I've had (guilty) fantasies about play like this for years, but I never thought it'd ever actually happen to me. And now that it is, I'm terrified that someone is going to realize what's going on and call us out on it. I glance around at the tables nearest us, but either I'm hiding it better than I think, or everyone's so involved with their own dinners and conversation that they don't seem to notice anything.

As if he's reading my mind, Keegan murmurs softly, "People are at their core pretty egotistical. Unless you make a disturbingly loud fuss, they're not going to notice that you can't sit still while I'm tormenting you." He grins, like that's supposed to be a positive. I suppose that in his world it is.

And he's not completely wrong. I'm so wet I'm worried the egg is going to slip right back out if I don't keep squeezing. Talk about incentive to keep up with your Kegels. If Mom wasn't there, I'd drag him home with me, because I'm so ready. He can take his ethics and shove them up his ass. Hell, if my Googling has taught me anything, prostate stimulation should only enhance things for him anyway.

I only barely make it through dinner. We talk, but I don't really remember much of it. I'm pretty sure that somewhere about halfway through he sped up the vibrations, but maybe I'm just getting oversensitive. At least we're close to the end, because if he expects to take me out dancing or anything crazy like that, he can forget it. I'd fall over.

Keegan scoops up the last of the sauce and risotto from his plate with a piece of focaccia, then sits back with his hands over his stomach. "Fuck, that was good. How was yours?"

My bowl is still half full. I take another forkful to double check the taste. "It's good. Sorry, I'm a little distracted."

He laughs. "Not too distracted, I hope. I wouldn't want you starving on my account."

I roll my eyes. It's nice that he's not one of those guys that judges every calorie I eat, but in spite of his games, I'm in no danger of starving. "No, I'm full. It was a pretty big portion. Maybe I should get a doggy bag."

"I'll ask the waitress to box it up. Ready for dessert?"

"Oh, I don't think I could eat another—"

"There's always room for a little gelato." That mischievous smirk tells me two things: one, it's not up for debate, and two, I'm not done with the commands yet. This time the shiver isn't from the little vibrator.

I bow my head. "Yes, Sir."

He reaches over the table and squeezes my hand at that. "Listen, I know you're new to this. If it's too much, you can stop anytime. Especially out here in public, with no warning, I don't demand the same type of obedience I do in the playroom."

Like it wasn't hot enough in here already. Thinking about the playroom makes me feel like someone just cranked the thermostat.

"We're just experimenting with different sorts of games, but I hope you're enjoying yourself. I don't want you to feel pressured, especially in an open environment like this."

I nod. I didn't really think that he would be mad if I'd said no, or refused to do anything he asked, but it's nice to get that confirmation. But, crazy as this is, and as frustrated I'm getting, I'm enjoying myself too. The attention, the danger. The fact that I'm finally daring to play the way I've fantasized about. Somehow, Keegan has won my trust, and I'm only too willing to let him have his way with me.

"I'm okay, Sir."

He squeezes my hand again, obviously pleased with my response.

The way he smiles, laughs, and now touches me, makes this date feel real, if it ever wasn't to begin with. At a distance, it's easy enough to agree that it's not right for us to be together, and potentially illegal to boot, but up close, all those concerns fade into the background so easily.

And I find myself not caring.

Our dinner is cleared away, and Keegan skips the dessert menu, directly requesting a couple of bowls of gelato. One raspberry and one vanilla.

I grin over at him. "I'm surprised you like anything vanilla."

He shrugs. "What can I say? It tastes good."

After a couple of minutes, the waitress is back with a couple of well-filled bowls. In addition to the gelato, there's a heaping bowl of fresh raspberries as well. It looks delicious. As soon as she's out of earshot, I look up at Keegan. "Man, everything's big here."

His face contorts like he's biting his tongue, holding back a comment.

"I know what you're thinking," I comment dryly while picking up my spoon.

"I didn't say anything," he protests.

"You didn't have to."

He laughs, and after a minute, I'm laughing too. It makes my core go tighter around the egg, intensifying the sensations and I gasp. When I get my senses back under control, I wag my finger at him. "Stop making me laugh."

"Not if I can help it." Picking up his dessert spoon, he scoops up a dollop of vanilla, captures a raspberry, and then leans towards me. "Open up."

"Wait, what?" I glance around, but no one's watching. "You're going to feed me?"

He just waits, the gelato thick on his spoon. I don't even have to ask if I'm blushing or not, since suddenly my face is as hot as my core. It's embarrassing, and just a little demeaning, and I have to figure out how I feel about that. Unbelievably, the simple act of opening my mouth for a spoonful of Italian ice cream is harder than anything he's put me through so far.

I mean, yeah, I've got the egg in me so this should be no big deal, right? It's not even so much kinky as it is public. He wants to feed me in front of all these people, making my submission obvious. My guilt and shame senses are tingling. I strongly suspect that when I'm looking back at tonight, this is going to haunt me. But I do it anyway.

Leaning towards him, I open my mouth and let him put a ridiculously rich and delicious spoonful in my mouth, the sweetness augmented by the tartness of the raspberry. Closing my lips around it, I look him right in the eyes and pull back, trying to make it as sexy as possible. From the fire that flares up in his eyes, I think I succeeded.

"Mmm," I moan, letting it coat my mouth in cool sweetness before swallowing. "That is really good. You should try some too," I venture while reaching for my own spoon.

Keegan laughs. "I'm doing the feeding here. At least this time." He takes a spoonful of the vanilla, with a raspberry, just like he served me. "Fuck, that is good. It's giving me some ideas for things to do that I can't do here. We'll just have to—"

He breaks off.

Evidently, I'm not the only one forgetting about ethics and restrictions and whatever reluctance we might have about this thing growing between us. I can't tell if this date was a great idea or just the ultimate exercise in frustration, but I'll enjoy while I've got it. Even if it goes no further, I'm having a great time.

Resigned, I nod at him. "I know. Sir."

Eyeing me dangerously, he takes another scoop, half raspberry, half vanilla. "Here."

Again, I let him feed it to me, pulling the delicious dessert off the spoon with my lips. After the mouthful slides coolly down my throat, I ask, "Are you really planning to feed me all of it? Sir?"

"No." He shakes his head. "I have a proposal instead." He reaches into his pocket and the vibration stops. As frustrating as it was, now I miss it. "I need you totally with me for this."

"Oh?"

"I know your mother is waiting at home—"

"Oh, don't say that. I'm having a good time. I swear." Knowing that the evening is nearing its end makes me dread going home all the more.

He nods, his expression serious as the grave. "Good. Come home with me."

"What?"

"I'll make sure you get home at a reasonable hour, but it's only nine fifteen. Come home with me, and I'll have you back by one, two tops." He takes my hand with both of his over the table, and squeezes. The depth of need in his eyes looks out of place on such a dominant man, but that makes it all the more poignant. "I know all the reasons this is a bad idea, but I can't fucking take it. I need you alone with me. I think we're both aware that this has gone way beyond any pretense at exposure therapy."

"I..."

"Please." Just that. A single word that puts the whole ball in my court.

It's up to me. I can go home with a good conscience, pretending that nothing serious happened. I'd regret it. I know I would. How would I feel about going home with him? What's he going to do to me? Would I regret that?

His hands are so warm, and I don't ever want him to let go. The way he looks at me, that naked desire—is my answer really in question?

"Yes."

A cautious smile spreads across his face. He flags down our waitress to get the check and five minutes later, we're in the back of a cab heading to his place, me tightly wrapped up in his arms and him kissing the top of my head.

Hopefully I made the right decision.

16

KEEGAN

Well, I've now officially crossed just about every line laid down by the rules of ethical behavior for psychologists. Or I'm about to. I never understood why people would risk their license before, but here I am, standing on the brink of a professional meltdown. Am I insane?

Instinctively, I squeeze Miranda tighter. I've probably gone off the deep end, but she drives me so crazy. All I can think about is her, and how I want her to be mine. Need her to be mine. Forget limiting our sessions to the office, I'll stop seeing her there at all. Anything we do from here out has to be purely private between me and Miranda.

Fuck, I should've ended the professional end of our relationship long ago, when I realized how fucking attracted I am to her. She's perfect. Funny, sexy, and just the right brand of submissive to drive me crazy. I need her in my life, and I think I can do good things for her.

I want what's best for her, to help her find the courage she needs to jump into the lifestyle with both feet. It's what she wants and I can help her.

Running my fingers through her hair, I marvel at its silky texture. She moans softly, pressing her face against my chest, as if she's trying to get closer to my heart.

Fuck, baby, you're already there.

The cab slows down and pulls over in front of my building. There's still time to stop this. To do the right thing and send her home, then break off contact, at least until she's worked through her remaining issues. I could find someone to refer her to, but while I'm sure they could talk about her family issues, I can't fucking imagine anyone else who can do this as well as I can. Guide her into a healthy relationship with BDSM.

The simple answer is I'd want to kill anyone else that tried.

But this has to be her choice, too.

Putting my curled index finger under her chin, I make her look up at me. The way her deep blue eyes bore into me, shining with excitement makes me want to kiss her instead of talk. I draw a breath, the sweet scent of her perfume tickling my nose. I almost don't ask at all, but I need to be sure, for her to be sure. There are no takebacks.

"Miranda, you don't have to do this. I want you to be sure. I'm your therapist, and that can make your feelings for me… complicated. If you're unsure at all, tell me now, because once we cross this line, we could be in a lot of trouble."

She nods. "I know. I googled it when I felt where we might be heading. I'm sure, but what about you? You'd be risking a lot. Does this feel right to you?"

"There's nothing I want more than to take you upstairs right now. Fuck everything else."

Licking her lips, she distracts me for a moment as I track the slow, sinewy movement of her tongue. And here I'm supposed to be the one in charge.

With a little nod, she seals our fate. "Let's do it."

The driver clears his throat. "Before you kids go off to do… whatever it is that you're getting ready to do, you still owe me eighteen fifty."

Oh Jesus Christ. When Miranda's here, everything fades away, easily forgotten. I laugh with a touch of embarrassment. "Yeah, of course. Here you go, keep the change." I hand him twenty-five bucks before popping the door.

"Thank you. You two have fun now."

Miranda laughs as I pull her out of the door behind me. "We will," she calls over her shoulder before pushing the door shut. We're up the steps to the front door before the car's even back out in traffic.

We take the elevator to the top floor, barely able to keep from stripping each other naked on the way up. Her ass is just too tempting, especially since I know there's nothing under her skirt. By the time we're outside my door, we're both breathing heavily and it takes a few tries to get the key in the lock.

As soon as we're inside, I slam the door behind me. Miranda doesn't even have time to take her coat off before I have her up against the wall and press my lips against hers. Now that we're finally doing this, I can't wait any fucking longer. I'm thirsting and she's my oasis.

Capturing her hands in mine, I pull them above her head and pin her wrists against the wall. She draws a sharp breath before I lean back in to trap her lower lip between my teeth. I press the length of my body against hers. My cock's aching in my pants, and I want her to feel it. To know how badly I want her.

Letting her lip slip, I trail kisses down her neck and onto her throat as she tilts her head back against the wall, exposing herself to me. I feel wild, like an animal, taking little bites at her pale skin. She moans in response, deep in her throat, and presses against me as much as she can while pinned by my body.

I've got to have her.

Stepping back, reluctant to break physical contact with her for even a second, I pull her with me by her wrists. She can get the grand tour later, but for now all we need is my bedroom.

"I don't think I can wait long enough to set up for a scene," I murmur while pulling her coat off and dropping it on the floor. "I've got to have you now."

Her hands are already at my pants, fiddling with my zipper as she shakes her head. "That's fine," she responds breathlessly.

Miranda gets my pants open, and then I'm pulling up at her clingy shirt. She raises her arms to help me, and as it comes off, her breasts bounce temptingly free, held only in place by a lacy black bra. I've still got the shirt in my hand, and inspiration strikes.

"Actually, I think we will play a little."

"What?"

Taking her wrists again, I bring her arms down behind her back, and pull her against me. She doesn't resist, though she sees quickly enough what I'm up to. In short order, her shirt's wrapped tightly around her wrists. Not as secure as ropes. If she wiggles enough, I'm sure she can break free, but it's good enough in a pinch. She tests it, but her hands go nowhere.

"Let me look at you." I crouch in front of her.

She still has her skirt on, though I already know there's nothing underneath. I'm about to unwrap her like it's Christmas and my birthday all at once. Reaching around to cup her ass with both hands, I pull her closer so I can kiss her belly button. Then I slowly stand, trailing a line of kisses up her stomach, between her breasts and along her collarbone. With every soft touch of my lips, a little shiver runs through her.

I slide my hands up her back, smiling when she squirms from the tickle, until I get to the catch of her bra. We both draw a breath as I unhook the band and let it slacken. The downside of her wrists being tied is that I can't pull it all the way up, but I'll work with it. "You're fucking beautiful," I whisper reverently as I pull the flimsy fabric aside and lock my lips around a pink nipple. I flick it with my tongue and she gasps.

She presses against me, struggling against her bonds while my hands roam up and down her sides. Their journey continues down her legs until I stop against her leather boots. They look so fucking sexy on her, I'm not taking those off. If I weren't rock hard already, the image of her in nothing except her boots would do it.

On the way back up, I go under her skirt, loving the sensation of her silky thigh-highs under my fingertips. Then I reach bare flesh and know I'm close. Following her soft thighs around, I cup her bare ass and squeeze possessively. She moans, but doesn't say anything, just watches me work.

I look her right in the eyes as I grip the hem of her skirt with both hands and start to lift slowly. She captures her lower lip in her teeth and watches me intently, her deep blues following my every move with a lot of heat and just a hint of trepidation. I kiss my way back down until I'm crouched in front of her, and then lift the skirt the rest of the way, baring her to me.

Fucking beautiful. Her sex is swollen with excitement, glistening wet and neatly trimmed, though the only thing that really matters is that it's hers, and she's excited to be with me. Leaning forward,

I place a soft kiss right where her excited clit pokes out of its hood. She gasps and draws back for a second before she straightens, back in position.

I kiss her again, and this time she stays put, even if she takes a sharp breath.

"Good girl," I hiss. Getting impatient, I unhook her skirt and toss it aside, leaving her for all practical purposes fully exposed. I stand and take a step back to soak in the view. Miranda's gorgeous, fucking gorgeous. Standing there with her back straight, her legs just a little bit spread with her hands tied behind her back. Leather boots, sexy garters, then nothing until her lacy bra which is hanging mostly off her sexy breasts. It's a look that's practically begging for sex, and I'm going to give her exactly what she deserves.

17

MIRANDA

K eegan steps back and eyes me so hungrily that he looks ready to eat me. Jade fire burns in his eyes as he looks me up and down. Trapped and naked, there's nothing I can do to stop him from helping himself to my body, and that has me dripping wet with anticipation.

I'm a defenseless Little Red Riding Hood and Keegan's the big bad wolf.

He wrenches off his jacket and throws it to the floor. Then he undoes his cufflinks and unbuttons the front of his crisp white shirt. I wet my lips as his powerful torso comes into view. He shucks the shirt off behind him, letting it pool to the floor. He's built like an athlete, tight muscles wrapped around his broad frame. Dark shadows outline his six-pack which tightens as he bends to finish undoing his pants.

"You're handsome, Sir," I breathe out to him.

He looks up and grins, his eyes glinting. "Then we're a good match, even if I'll never live up to how incredibly beautiful you are."

And here I didn't think my face could feel any warmer.

He pulls his pants down, revealing black boxer briefs and a bulge that makes me want to run over and yank them down, but my hands are tied.

Kicking off his shoes, he makes short work of his socks and pants. Then he hooks his thumbs into the elastic of his underwear. Giving me a confident smirk, he pulls, but also bends over so I can't see what he's exposing. Not until he straightens and steps out of the briefs puddled at his feet.

Wow.

Standing straight and pointing right at me, his thick cock twitches as he flexes. He crooks his finger, summoning me. "Come show me how badly you want it."

I feel like I'm licking my lips an awful lot today, but I can't help it. Taking the few steps between us, I stop right in front of him and carefully get down on my knees. He supports me with his hands so I won't fall, and then I'm there, facing him, up close and personal.

I'm no virgin, but I'll be honest, I'm not super experienced with blowjobs either. I want to help with my hands, but I can't, so I do my best, sliding my tongue slowly along his smooth length, inwardly smiling when he hisses in reaction. Up along the front, then I swirl around the head. The salty flavor of his precum mingles with clean skin while I tease right along the rim of his crown. I rise up on my knees and take the whole head, slowly and wetly fucking him with my mouth.

"Oh, that's good," he groans in a raspy voice.

I have a moment of pride at being able to make him feel that way. Somehow I'm in control, even if he's standing over me and I'm the one with my hands tied behind my back.

He's so thick. And this is supposed to go inside me? It's going to be a tight fit, but I want to feel him pulsing deep in my core, the same way I feel his heartbeat against my tongue.

He slides his hands into my hair, fisting it between his fingers. With his strong grip, he helps me, guiding me where he wants me, slowly fucking my mouth. He flexes his hips and pushes deeper, not so far that I can't handle it, but more than I might've on my own. Then out again, then in, over and over. His breath is short, staccato, like he's working out, but his hips thrust and pull back in a slow and measured fashion. His eyes are on me the whole time.

I feel owned. Here for his pleasure. It goes against everything I've ever been taught, but on some level, buried deep in my primitive lizard-brain, I know I need this. It's something that I've always craved, but never quite understood how to get and how to feel about. Now Keegan is showing me exactly what he wants, and it's turning out to be exactly what I want.

Suddenly he pulls me off. "Jesus, too much more of that, and this'll all be over. I'm not ready for that." He grins. "You're amazing, Miranda. Just fucking amazing. Here." Putting his hands under my armpits, he raises me up to my feet as if I weigh nothing.

"Thank you, Sir," I mumble. I've never been good at taking compliments, and the way he showers them on me is overwhelming.

He laughs. "No, thank you. I think it's time I return the favor. Come here." With his hands on my upper arms, he guides me to the bed and bends me over it. It's so tall that I'm hardly bending my knees at all. Without my hands to catch me, I lie there flat, my cheek against the sheets.

"Nice," he compliments, "But I need your knees up on the edge." Putting one hand under my right knee, he lifts it up to give me the idea. Then the other leg, so that now I'm face down on his bed with my ass in the air, and he has a completely unobstructed view of my everything.

I feel really exposed, and without my hands to support me, I can't even really move around to see what he's doing without getting out of position.

The first sign of what he's planning is his hands on the backs of my thighs, gripping them firmly, just below where they meet my ass, his thumbs nearly touching my pussy. The second is his breath blowing over me, right between my legs, where I need him the most. He starts with a tease, kissing my thighs and my ass, all the time tantalizingly close to where I want him, but never quite getting there.

After what seems like an eternity of torment, I can't stand it any longer. "Please, Sir."

He stops his kisses long enough for me to imagine the cocky smirk on his lips. "Please what? Tell me what you want."

Oh God, I can't actually say it out loud. "Please, Sir. I'm begging."

"Mmm, yes you are, and that's got my cock hard as a fucking rock, but I want you to ask me nicely exactly what you want me to do."

That bastard. He resumes his kissing all around, so close that sometimes his nose brushes against my folds, but then he pulls back just as fast. I'm on fire, and he's refusing to put it out. In the end, I submit.

"Please, lick me. Sir."

"Lick you where?"

I swallow. "Please lick my pussy, Sir."

"Now that's what I wanted to hear," he replies hungrily, and then his broad tongue laves a wide swath between my legs, the tip flicking over my clit as it slides past. God, he's good at that.

And again. With his thumbs, he pulls me open, exposing my innermost parts to his soothing tongue. He doesn't put out the fire, but his touch is a relief, a progression which leads to an end, instead of being trapped by his teasing.

With his strength, he pushes me forward, tilting my hips for better access, then fluttering his tongue across my clit in a maddening pattern. It's like he already knows where my buttons are and exactly how to push them. As his tongue tracks across my sensitive skin, I wiggle my hips to follow until his grip tightens to hold me in place.

"Easy, baby. Only when I'm ready."

He's almost got me begging again in no time. Every cell in my body aches for release, and while he pushes me closer and closer, every time I think it's going to happen, he backs off and starts over again.

"You're a tease!" I call out, and get rewarded with a thorough swat on my ass.

Keegan laughs at my surprised yelp. "Proper address. And no abusing your master."

"Yes, Sir," I whimper, with no idea what to do. If I move I get punished, but much more of this teasing and I'm going to go out of my mind.

Finally, he slips his tongue back where I want it while his hands roam all over my ass and thighs. Risking another swat, I press back against him, but he just continues on at his own pace. My thighs shake from tension and I squeeze my eyes tightly together. A ripple begins somewhere near my pussy, tightening all of my muscles until I'm a bow string ready to be released.

Just a little more.

He knows. And to my relief, he seems ready to give me the payoff, because his tongue starts to work overtime on my clit, sliding quickly back and forth over my tingling nub. My moans barely make it through my constricted diaphragm, my tension so high I'm sweating.

There's a soft pressure against my asshole. His thumb, I realize with surprise. Nothing deep, but massaging it, the tip sometimes slipping just inside. No one's ever done that to me, but after a moment's surprise, it's the final bit of stimulation that sets me off.

An intense heat washes over me and I groan loudly into the sheets. My trapped hands make fists, then open, only to fist again, wanting to clutch at something, anything, while my orgasm makes my body tremble. My stomach is so tight it aches, and yet I'm pressing against him with a need to ride these sensations for as long as they'll last.

I might have passed out for a second, but I'm still up on my knees, so maybe it just feels that way. But now it's too much. "Please, too sensitive. Sir."

He laughs, and even that gentle puff of air tickles my clit in a way that's deliciously unbearable. With a last wet kiss on my folds that sends tendrils of shivers through all of me, he finally backs off and lets me flop over onto my side, half on, half off the bed. "I've wanted to do that since I met you," he rumbles as he drops onto the bed next to me. It's impossible not to notice that he's still hard as a rock and pointing in my direction.

He'll have to wait a little longer, since right now I feel so liquid that I'm a puddle on his sheets, unable to go anywhere except mold myself to the softness of his bed. "Thank you, Sir," I whisper.

Reaching over, he runs his fingers lightly up and down my side. His cock twitches, blood red and the tip slick with precum. By all signs, he's showing amazing restraint by not just rolling me over and plunging inside.

My breathing slows and the aftershocks of my orgasm fade until he's not the only one ready for more. I spread my legs for him. "You look like there's more you'd like to do." I meet his smoldering gaze as he looks up at me. "Sir," I tack on.

No more invitation is necessary. He rolls me roughly over onto my stomach, and surprisingly, releases my arms. "I want you on your back, so you can look at me while I fuck you senseless," he growls.

Oh God.

Flipping me over again so quickly I shriek, he pulls my ass right to the edge of the bed and looms over me. His cock hovers, practically vibrating with readiness, right above my pussy.

Taking my ankles, Keegan brings them up to his broad shoulders, then he takes my wrists and crosses them over my head in one large hand, so I'm trapped beneath him. He leans in until the broad head of his cock brushes against my folds. "Okay?" is all he asks, looking right into my eyes.

My gaze never leaves his as I nod. "Okay."

He holds himself above me, the corded muscles in his arms tense. With his free hand, he takes himself and slides the tip up and down through my slick folds, never quite making it in. I groan in frustration, but he's got me completely pinned. He grins. "You didn't say Sir."

God, what a control freak. I'd be mad if I didn't love it so much. "Okay, Sir." I put extra emphasis in the word. "Please, Sir."

"Fuck, that's exactly what I needed to hear." He sinks into me, slowly, deliberately, filling completely. I close my eyes and try to keep my breathing steady. He's not having any of it. "Look at me while I fuck you."

My eyes pop open at his command, staring right into his intense gaze. My legs are spread wide open by his broad shoulders, and his hand is like a hot brand around my wrists. He's so much larger than I am that I'm helpless, completely in his power, and it doesn't matter that there're no ropes or chains binding me. Even if he weren't holding me down, I couldn't walk away.

I'm exactly where I want to be, right here, right now.

Keegan's angular hips press against the backs of my thighs. He's all the way in, huge and hard. Big enough that I'm a little proud for taking all of him. In this position, he's so deep it'd require gentleness even if he weren't so endowed, but despite the spanking and flogging and ordering around, his actual penetration has been exactly that. Gentle. Even now, he's just there, all the way in and letting me get used to him being there.

But I want to be fucked.

"I'm okay, Sir. Do what you want to do."

He smiles. "But I *am* doing what I want to do." Then he leans even further down, making me glad I'm pretty flexible. Far enough that he can touch his lips to mine in a soft kiss. "I want you under me like this all the time. Every fucking day."

"I think we'd both get fired."

He laughs, and it transfers straight from his body into mine via his cock. Even that gets a sharp breath out of me. What is actually fucking going to be like? "You're probably right," he admits. "But then we'll just have to make each of these moments all the sweeter."

He pulls back, leaving a void that's just aching for his return. Right up until just the tip of him is inside, then he presses forward, harder and faster than the first time, pushing the breath right out of me.

"Yes, Sir," I gasp between strokes.

His muscles work tirelessly as he moves faster and harder. Watching him is captivating, the way his shoulders flex, how his eyes follow my every movement, and how he leans in to kiss my lips while he works himself in and out of me. I'm trapped for him to use, and he uses me so well. It's not long before the heat builds in my core and my body tingles. I have to agree, I could live with this being my life.

"You feel so good." Keegan groans into my ear, putting his weight on me and really starting to thrust. The bedroom is filled with the sounds of flesh against flesh as he fucks me. He captures a lobe between his teeth, the sharp pressure a faint sting in my lust-induced haze.

I love the way he dominates me and want to wrap my arms around him, to cling to him and let my nails dig into his back as he drives me crazy with his long powerful strokes. But it doesn't really matter what I want, because right now, I'm his to do with as he pleases. It's a good thing that what pleases him is to please me.

I wriggle and grind beneath him, not trying to escape, but unable to lie still while all these wonderful sensations course through me. My body tightens up, that familiar rush filling me again as I flow towards the precipice, ready to let the rush of another orgasm fling me over the edge.

Keegan's not far behind. He moans from deep in his throat, growing louder in time with his thrusts. He's still looking in my direction, but his eyes have taken on a faraway look as he loses himself. We race, grinding against each other as we fuck, both of us charging towards that ultimate goal together.

I win, barely. Only seconds after my own climax knocks me over like a tidal wave, he rears like a stallion, his muscular abs straining as he pours himself into me in pulse after pulse. I quiver beneath him, every muscle in my body clenching around him, milking him dry and unwilling to ever let go.

For several long moments, my world is nothing but colors and lights as I writhe in orgasm. His thickness throbs inside me, and his heavy breathing is a soft rush over my skin. It feels like I'm submerged in thick, warm, comforting fluid, completely safe and sated.

When I become aware of my surroundings again, Keegan's right there, above me... in me. He smiles. "Welcome back."

I blink a couple of times. A deep breath, and then I think I can talk. "Hi."

He slides slowly out, before rolling both of us over so we're lying on our sides, facing each other. Tracing my hair with his hand, all the way down along my face, he hooks it where my neck meets the back of my head and pulls me in for a kiss. To be honest, I don't need any pulling. The crazy intensity of our sex has simmered down, but the soft touches of our lips in the aftermath are nice too.

"So, glad you came home with me?" he asks once we've separated. He runs a finger teasingly down my side from under my arm to my hips.

I nod with a swallow. "Yeah. Not bad."

"Not bad?" he responds in mock anger. I grin back at him, though it turns more into a grimace when his strong hand comes down hard on my ass. The slap echoes slightly.

"Okay, okay, it was wonderful. Amazing. The best sex of my life."

He laughs. "Now you're patronizing me." He lands a second slap, right where the previous one hit.

"No! Honest." I stop to draw a breath and calm myself so I can sound serious. "Really, I mean it. It was amazing. You're all that I hoped and so much more."

I half expect another smart-alecky remark and another spank, but instead he looks at me intently. "Thank you," he replies without a trace of sarcasm or irony. "It was pretty fucking amazing."

"God, what time is it?" Suddenly I remember I've got someone waiting at home.

He glances at his night stand. "About ten thirty. Not too bad. Time for a post-coital cuddle?"

I nod. "Yeah, that sounds good."

He wraps his arms around me and pulls me close. I curl up around his side, my head resting on his chest and one leg thrown across his waist. He's so warm and comfortable, it's like I was meant to fit around him.

A billion things are bouncing around my head. First things first: I had kinky sex. Nothing super wild, but he tied me up, positioned me… I called him Sir, and I feel good. Maybe I'm still high on endorphins, but there's no guilt, no shame, no flashbacks that I'd rather forget. Just me. And a feeling of belonging.

Absentmindedly, I place a couple of kisses on Keegan's chest, and he responds by running his fingers softly up and down my back. I trust him. Maybe that's all I was missing? I couldn't do this with just any man, just play like Amber wanted me to, but with Keegan it all seems so different. I'm not afraid of him.

The thought makes me smile as I close my eyes and luxuriate in the comfort of his arms.

18

MIRANDA

Mmm, my bed's nice and warm. I snuggle deeper into the covers, enjoying the luxury of waking up slowly. No nightmares today. It already feels like it's going to be a good day. I roll over, dragging the sheets with me and bump into... someone?

My eyes pop open in surprise. Looking right at me, looking just as bleary-eyed and disoriented is—

"Keegan! What are you doing in my—" I was going to say room, but it doesn't take long to realize this isn't my room at all. Last night comes back to me in a furious rush of vivid images, sinful sensations and sexy taste of the forbidden. What doesn't quite come back to me is why I'm still here, waking up in Keegan's bed when I should've been home hours ago.

Shit, how many hours ago? "What time is it?"

He sits up, the sheets dropping down to reveal his cut torso. There's a strong part of me that considers not worrying about the time after all, and jumping him instead. He's so gorgeous, and he's mine. What's another hour going to matter, right?

"Eight thirty-two," he mumbles, blinking groggily. "I don't have an appointment until ten thirty, so I'm good."

"Crap. I've been gone the whole night, and I have a shift starting at ten. I'm never going to make it." I throw the sheet off and jump out of bed, and then remember that I'm bare-ass naked.

Keegan laughs when I try to cover up with my hands. "There isn't a square inch of that body I didn't explore last night. You're not going shy on me now, are you?"

"No, I mean—maybe? Where are my clothes? I need to get home. If I rush, maybe I'll make it."

Admitting to myself that modesty is pretty silly at this point, I scavenge any garments I can find off the floor. Skirt, bra, my blouse over a chair. Panties? Oh right, in his suit jacket. My stockings have a run in them, but I'm just going home. I ball them up and stuff them in my purse to throw out later.

"I'll drive you." He throws the sheets aside and hops out of bed, totally unconcerned about his cock swinging free, as naked as I am. Well, was, as I zip up my skirt. Opening a closet, he pulls out fresh underwear, a clean shirt and a pair of dark jeans.

We dress quickly, Keegan looking stylish and neat, his five o'clock shadow only adding to his sexiness. Me, on the other hand, I'm sporting the latest in walk of shame chic, still in yesterday's makeup and stiff from... I shiver from the memory of the night before, not to mention all the times we woke up during the night and he filled me up with his giant cock. No wonder I'm a little sore.

Happy, but a little sore and a lot late.

"All right, are you ready? Wait, where are my keys?" He stops and thinks. "Ah, fuck. My car's still at the restaurant. I'll order a ride." He grabs his phone.

"It's okay. You don't have to come." I look around to make sure I have everything. I don't even want to look in a mirror. "God, I'm a mess."

"You're beautiful. If we weren't in a hurry, I'd throw you right back onto that bed and fuck you silly." He opens the door and, rolling my eyes, I follow as quickly as I can. A minute later, the Uber pulls up to the curb.

"Seriously, I'm fine by myself. We'll talk after work."

"Bullshit. If I'm in trouble for bringing you home late, I'll own up to it. You're not taking all the blame. It was both of us."

"No, really. It's fine. There'll be less yelling and stress this way. It's going to be difficult enough to deal with Mom and still make it to work on time without you being there to make it more complicated."

"Miranda."

"No, I'll be fine." I give him a smile, trying to be encouraging.

"This is the mother that's the source of your complexes that I'm supposed to be helping you with, right?" His disagreement is plainly visible in his expression.

"Yeah, but, not now. She'll be angry, I'm sure, but I'm an adult and I can't handle it. God knows it's not the first time I've done something she didn't approve of. It'll be fine." If I say it enough, I might just believe it myself.

He sighs. "If you're sure. Listen, I'm a phone call away, alright? If things get rough and you need to get out of there, or just want someone to help mediate, don't hesitate to let me know."

That gets me smiling, and my heart warming. "I appreciate that."

"I have appointments on and off all day, so at least text me to let me know you make it into work."

"Alright, alright. I get it. You want to take care of me." I lean in for a quick kiss, but instead he grabs me behind my neck and makes it a long, passionate one. When I finally get up for air, I shake my head. "Wowee. If that's what I've been missing all this time, then I'm totally okay with this new state of our relationship."

He laughs. "Okay, go, before I change my mind."

Popping the door, I slide into the car, then give him a quick wave. "Bye."

"Bye." He's still waving as my car pulls out.

We're going to have to have a real talk, and soon. Last night completely blew any distance we were meant to keep way out of the water. Neither of us had planned for it, though we definitely put ourselves in a position to lose control over and over again. So maybe his subconscious wanted it as much as I know mine did.

Look at me, psychoanalyzing the analyst.

Traffic's light for a change and I'm home almost before I know it. Everything's already paid for by Keegan, so as soon as I'm dropped off, I rush up to my apartment a warp speed.

My key isn't even in the door when mom rips it open. "Where have you been, young lady?" Her brows are deeply furrowed, and her mouth a thin straight line. "You were supposed to come home last night. I've been so worried. Did he take advantage of you? He did, didn't he?"

I hold my hands up to stem her angry word flood. "God, Mom. Why do you always have to jump to the worst conclusions? He didn't kidnap and rape me if that's what you're asking. We're two adults who enjoyed each other's company. I lost track of time and ended up crashing at his place. I'm sorry I didn't call, but I swear I'm fine."

Taking my wrist, she drags me into my own apartment and slams the door. "Don't act so flippant with me. I was half expecting to have the police come knocking, telling me they'd found your body in a gutter somewhere."

"And here I thought you liked Keegan. I can only imagine what you would've thought if he'd been someone you didn't like."

She snorts. "You wouldn't have made it out the door. Which is apparently what I should've done yesterday, too."

"I'm twenty-two! I can take care of myself." I almost feel bad for snapping at her when I see the hurt look on her face. I'm not really in a habit of speaking up or getting angry because it's easier to let her overbearing tendencies slide so I don't have to deal with them, but when mom jumps all over Keegan, it puts me on the defensive. This isn't just about me, it's about him. "You've gone completely overboard. Keegan was a perfect gentleman the whole time, the kind who respects the woman he's with and treats her the way she deserves."

In my case that was tied up, spanked and well fucked, but in broad strokes we're in agreement here. Then I get thinking about broad things stroking, and I have to refocus.

Mom deflates a little in the face of my defiance. "I couldn't know that, Miranda. You were just gone, and you didn't let me know what was going on."

"You could've called if you were that worried."

"I tried! Several times and you didn't answer. What did you expect me to think?"

I dig for my phone in my purse. Of course the battery's dead. Didn't I charge it before going out last night? "Okay, I'm sorry. My phone's dead." I sigh. "That's my fault, but you don't have to jump straight to assuming he's some kind of serial murderer."

She wraps her arms around me and pulls me closer. "I'm your mother. I worry about you. You know that."

"Sure, Mom, but some day you need to accept that I've grown up."

"You're right, but it isn't easy. You've grown into a strong woman, and I'm proud of you, but I'm never going to stop wanting to protect you. I don't want you to fall for the same kinds of things that I did at your age. Every time you're out with someone, I'm terrified."

I sigh, understanding where she's coming from, but not knowing how to get through to her. "Don't let how Dad treated you run both our lives. He wasn't good to you. To us. Keegan's not like him."

"Brad started out wonderful too. It didn't stop him in the long run."

"Sometimes you just have to take the risk. Keegan treats me well. He makes me feel good. He respects me and my decisions. You were ready to give him a chance last night. He hasn't done anything to change that, all right?" I grip mom's arm just below the shoulder, squeezing for emphasis. "I like him. Please don't ruin this for me."

She refuses to meet my gaze, which is unlike her. "I'll try to keep my worries to myself, but if you go out again while I'm here, you make sure your phone's charged."

"Of course, Mom. I'm sorry." I smile, trying to reassure her. "Now, I have to hurry and get ready for work. I'm already going to be late if I don't get a serious move on. I'd stay and talk, but I already tried to get the time off when I found out you were coming and there's nobody to cover me."

She nods. "Of course. But if any of those customers give you any trouble, you let me know and I'll sit there with my knitting and scare them off."

Sheesh, why do all the people in my life seem to think I need round the clock care? "Sure, Mom. I'm going go to shower and then I have to run."

She nods, returning to my couch and settling down in front of the TV with her knitting. I'll have to have a longer talk with her, too. We can't keep doing this. I'm starting to think she's the one that really needs counseling, and not just the kind she gets with Gladys and the other women back home.

Okay, work.

Twenty minutes later, I'm showered, dressed, hastily made up and rushing for the door.

"Love you, baby," Mom yells from the couch.

"You too," I reply over my shoulder.

19

KEEGAN

Well, fuck, I don't know what to do. That's a feeling I'm neither used to nor particularly fond of. After back to back sessions well into the afternoon, a late lunch is order, and while it's not particularly fancy, the bar food at the club sounds just about perfect. It would also help to have a chat with someone who might understand my predicament. I could do the macho thing and bottle it all up until it all goes wrong, but I picked the wrong profession if I didn't want to know how dumb that is.

At this hour, the club's pretty quiet. There's a DJ setting up to host tonight's party, but other than that, only the bar is seeing any activity. A couple is having cocktails in the lounge, probably preparing for an early start, and there's a woman at the bar sipping fizzy water while having a burger. At the end of the bar, some guy is nursing a beer. And then there's me.

Gabe steps up as I slip onto a bar stool. He pats me on the shoulder with a grin. "Keegan. What's up? Business good?"

"Yeah, booming. I still appreciate that you've recommended me to the members here. It's drummed up a bunch of business, and hopefully I've managed to help a few souls find their way in the process."

"From what I hear, you've only left me with happy customers. That's a win-win, in my book."

I nod, glad to hear it. "Good. How's Dawn? Doing well? Hell, how's life with a little pudding?"

Gabe laughs. "It's a whole new world. Suddenly I'm the damn sub, running around at the beck and call of a little beast who only knows how to scream, eat and shit. But I'm loving it. Dawn's doing well too. Exhausted, but happy. We're making it work."

"That's great. Listen, do you have time for a chat? I could do with some advice."

He glances around the bar. "Sure. Things are still pretty quiet. It's more fun at night, of course, but while the baby's still small I'd rather be home to help out in the evenings."

"Yeah, I get that. Could I have a Coke? I need to drive back to work after."

"Sure thing." Gabe pours a glass and sets it in front of me. "On the house."

"Oh, I can't—"

"It's just syrup and water, man." Gabe grins. "Don't worry about it. So what does a therapist need advice about?"

"Thanks." I tip the glass at him in a toast before taking a sip. The punch of sweetness reminds me of Miranda and her hot chocolate. She texted me a while ago to let me know she made it to work, but I can't help thinking about her and wondering how she's doing. "Okay, here's the deal, and just for the record, I'm trusting you not to screw me over with this information." I take a deep breath. "I've fallen for someone."

He gives me a confused but curious look. "Okay… grats, but I'm guessing there's more to it than that."

"She's a client, from here."

His eyes narrow and he leans back against the counter. It's obvious he's not thrilled with that admission. "There are rules about that, aren't there?"

"Yeah, lots of them," I reply grimly. "If I were advising a friend, I'd tell him to back the hell out."

"So back the hell out."

I roll the cold glass back and forth between my palms. "It's not that easy."

"You're going to have to give me more to go on, man. I appreciate that you came to me, but I trusted you by recommending your services to the members. That's not something I can do if you're using it as some kind of fucked up dating service."

"Oh for Christ's sake, you know I wouldn't do that," I snap, looking up to find him watching me with a look that's more understanding than angry. "I wouldn't do that."

"I know, but why don't you tell me what's going on."

"One of the newbies Amber took under her wing called me up a while back. We… we hit it off right from the start. And that's never, *never*, happened to me before with a client. I thought I could handle it, but she feels it too, and even though it's both unethical and illegal for me to pursue anything with her…"

"Maybe you should talk to Paul. You know him? Paul Cannon."

I shake my head. "Nope."

"I'll introduce you later. He's a cop and might be able to give you some more practical advice, but for now I'll play TV shrink and throw this back in your face. What do you think is the right thing to do?"

I roll my eyes at him and take a drink. "If I knew that, I wouldn't be here, would I?"

"Really? You have no idea? You seemed pretty sure about what you'd advise your friend." There's an amused glint in Gabe's eyes.

With soft laugh, I curl my lip at him. "Fuck you."

"So, obviously, you know what the right thing to do is, but let me guess. She's pulling every string to appeal to you as a client, a woman and a submissive. Not an easy thing to ignore. Especially since guys like us get off on control and caring for the vulnerable people in our lives."

"Honestly, I'm surprised you haven't run into this problem before. Before Dawn, I would've been a goner the first time a beautiful women walked into the room and told me to make it better. There must be something different about this one."

I slam my hand on the bar. "Exactly. Usually, I'm okay. I like helping people. So far, it's never been a problem, and you know that.

"But…"

With a sigh, I finish for him, "But with her, it's become a real struggle, and one I lost last night."

He frowns. "So this isn't just theoretical, then. How does she feel about it?"

"She's in love. Fuck, she's doing everything she can to draw me in. I can't talk about her details, obviously. Client confidentiality, but obviously there's a reason she came to me in the first place. Given the nature of how we met, there's a distinct possibility she's more in love with the idea of me, rather than with the actual me." I spin my glass in place, watching the Coke swirl while I work through my thoughts.

"Well, you know how this works. Communication is key. In the bedroom as much as the playroom. Talk to her."

"Yeah, I try, but it's awfully distracting. I go in full of good intentions, and then suddenly we're naked, she's tied up and we're going to town."

This time, Gabe barks out a surprised laugh. "Fuck, man, you've got it bad."

Over a sip, I nod. "Tell me about it."

There's a bit of a pause before he sighs. "All right, listen. I'm generally a live and let live kind of guy. I don't encourage breaking the law, but I've stretched a few here and there in my life. Ask Dawn how we met sometime." He grins at some private recollection. "But here's a question for you. Are you sure you're not abusing your power?

You've found someone who gets you all fired up, and maybe, just maybe, has you overlooking the fact that she also needs help. That's why she came to you in the first place."

"You're absolutely right. That's the most dangerous part. If I lose my license, I fuck my own life up, but if I fuck hers up, that's a whole other story. That would be not only failing at my job, but failing her. We're so closely entangled, it's hard to tell where the professional ends and the personal starts."

"So you should quit her then."

Probably, but I'm not sure I can at this point. "I've helped her. I'm *helping* her. I know I am. She's getting more confident, and she's... well, she's responding and moving in the right direction. Our relationship, at least in this case, is helping her get where she wants and providing her with a safe haven to land in at the same time."

"So it is a problem or not? If she's happy, and you're happy, are you maybe just overthinking things?"

"That's what I want to think. She won't get out of my head, and the longer she's there, the less I want her to. We help the people we love, don't we? That only makes it better."

Gabe reaches over the bar to put his hand on my shoulder. "For what it's worth, I think life's too short to give up on true love." At my look, he grins. "So sue me, I'm a fucking romantic. Now, I'll freely admit that this is probably not sensible advice, but meeting the right one is pretty fucking special. If you really think that's her, well… I'd at least consider giving it a try. But that's me, not you."

"So you don't think I'm nuts?"

"Jury's out on that one." He grins. "But ask yourself this. Is this what's best for her? Or are you just rationalizing because you don't want to let go?" A small group of older kinksters come in and settle around one of the tables. Gabe waves to them. "Anyway, got to help these people out. I'm sure you've got plenty to think about, anyway."

"Yeah, don't worry about it. Thanks."

"Good luck, man. I think you're going to need it."

Now that's the truth. My phone buzzes, and I pull it out absentmindedly. It's a message from Miranda.

I'm almost done at work. Is it too soon to ask for a repeat of last night? ;)

Images of a naked and moaning Miranda flash briefly through my head. Just long enough to make my pants go tight. Fuck yeah, I'd love a repeat. That's not in question. But should I?

My training screams no.

My cock demands yes.

And my heart doesn't know what the fuck to do. But I definitely know which part of my body it's the busiest pumping blood to right now. *Up for a night at the club? A BDSM date for real?*

Her reply is almost immediate. *Friday night? I have a late shift tomorrow, and I promised Mom we'd spend tonight together.*

I could still back out. *Sounds great. I'll pick you up.*

But I obviously won't.

How about I meet you there? I have a surprise planned for you, but I won't be able to show you at home. ;)

With that kind of cliffhanger, there's no way I'm backing out now. This girl's going to be the end of me.

I just hope I don't return the favor.

20

MIRANDA

The powerful sound system at the club thrums with heavy bass beats that reverberate in the core of my gut and threaten to bounce my breasts right out of my dress. It drives the sexualized melee on the dance floor, while colored lights flit back and forth, lighting the dancers in intricate patterns that match the rhythm of the music. As usual, the dress code spans from formal to nothing at all, and everything in between. Friday nights are a madhouse, when not only the regulars show up in force, but all the weekend warriors start to make their appearances too. Normally I prefer when it's not quite so crowded, but tonight is special.

I have a date. In a BDSM club.

I even dressed the part, and Keegan had better appreciate it. Wearing this outfit in public is spiking my anxiety through the roof. The woman at the coat check had to nearly pry my coat from my fingers. I was so close to chickening out.

Very self-consciously, I tug the hem of my black latex mini-dress, which clings to my curves like Saran Wrap. It made me feel like a bondage queen in front of the mirror at home, but now I worry that I'm showing just a little more bulge than I should be. It keeps riding up my thighs, but when I pull it down, I'm terrified that I'm going to pop right out on top. Add in a pair of latex gloves that go up past my elbows, knee-high leather boots with thick heels and buckles all over the place and a sturdy leather collar with a steel ring in front, and you get a woman who's dressed to kill but feeling really awkward about it.

Keegan's jaw drops when he sees me. He's waiting inside the door and when he looks me up and down, I can see him trying to decide which part to eat up first. "Holy fuck," he lets out. The hungry look on his face blasts away all my awkwardness.

I rub my lips together, feeling the silky slide of my red lipstick. "Did I do okay?"

He grins like a starving wolf. "Oh yeah, you did. If you don't come with me right now, I'm going to pick you up and carry you off to our room. You look fucking amazing."

Maybe I should've warned him, so he could've put on something to match. Then again, it's not like he isn't looking great. No suit today, but the way those jeans hug his leg and his tight gray T-shirt stretches across his broad chest... well, I'm sure not complaining. His hair is slightly mussed, but probably very much on purpose, and he's cleanly shaven for that smooth feeling when he's down between my legs.

Oh, I did not just think that.

Oh, yes I did.

I press my face into his chest so he won't see me blush. "And I'm going to have to fight off every other woman here on the way to the playroom so nobody steals you away."

He laughs, his chest rumbling in my ear. "No chance of that."

"And my outfit, it's not too—"

"It's not too anything." He hooks a finger under my chin and tilts my face up to his. With a sinful smile, he closes in for a kiss. It's warm and wet and sexy and *everything*. The desire in his touch gets my heart racing.

When he pulls away, I have to catch my breath. "We have a room?"

"You bet your sweet ass we do."

"Lead on." Adrenaline already has my heart pounding. And a bit lower, too. I lick my lips, loving how his eyes follow the motion of my tongue, and then I tack on, "Sir."

He doesn't say anything, just holds my upper arm with a steel grip and steers me along. Not that I need the encouragement, because I follow him eagerly.

My stomach tumbles over and over, like a butterfly colony doing somersaults. This is it. The real thing. I never thought I'd dare to do this. It's a biggest middle finger ever raised to my insecurities, fears and most of all, to my father's painful legacy. I'm going in there with Keegan, not with therapy as an excuse, but just because I want to.

If that's not an achievement, I don't know what is.

We squeeze through the dancefloor. Today it's so packed that not even Keegan's broad shape can keep a path open for long. I feel like an envelope from Amazon forced through the mail slot by an overzealous mailman. I get through, but maybe a bit ruffled at the edges.

Despite my excitement, I'm also terrified. Now that I've finally gotten what I wanted, what if I screw it up? Or what if I can't handle it? I trust Keegan, but this has gone almost too smoothly.

He glances over his shoulder to make sure I'm keeping up, and gives me a reassuring smile. I smile back. I shouldn't worry. This is going to be fine. I've got it under control.

Even the corridor is crowded tonight. We come out into the play area so suddenly, I half expect to hear the pop. At least once we're in, there's a bit more room to move. There's a demo on the center stage, a long-haired woman demonstrating shibari macramé. She's woven her curvy model a complete set of underwear from brightly colored purple and neon green rope. The model twirls on the stage to show off her outfit while the audience claps. Impressive, and normally I'd be standing there watching with the rest of them, but I'm having a hard time tearing my gaze away from Keegan.

Amber bears down on us out of left field, tearing me out of Keegan's grasp and wrapping her arms around me in a laughing bear hug before she pulls back, holding me at arm's length by my shoulders. "Oh my God, look at you. You're gorgeous!" I don't even get a word in before she barrels on. "I knew it. I told you so. I totally did."

I can't contain the laugh. "Fine. Okay. You did. Are you happy now?"

She glances briefly at Keegan before she looks back at me, giving me the once over. "Yeah. I think I am. Anyway, Eric's on his way over, and I want to grab a playroom before they fill up, so I'm going to leave you kids to your fun." She stops long enough to take both of my hands in hers and pull me into another hug. "I'm so proud of you."

"You're crazy," I laugh but I hug her back.

Keegan wraps his strong arms around me as Amber walks away. "You know, I'm a little surprised you wanted to come here so soon," he says into my hair before kissing the top of my head.

"Why? I was the one who asked you, remember?"

"I know, but this is a big step. You've been watching this from the outside for a long time. It has to be strange to finally be taking part." His grip tightens, as if I might run. "But you're here. Amber's not the only one who's proud of you."

"Good thing I'm cured, right?" I grin up at him, while I run my fingers over the front of his T-shirt, tracing the tight muscles hiding underneath.

He smiles, but it looks a little unsure. "I still think we should try to take it slow. I don't want you trading old problems for new ones."

I'm not crazy about him giving voice to my doubts. Not that he's doing anything wrong, but I've been trying to push them to the back of my mind. My anxiety is prone to assaulting my confidence and stuffing it into a closet, like some sort of brain home invader. If I let my doubts free, I'm going to back out, and I don't want to.

It's funny. A couple of weeks ago, you couldn't have dragged me into the private rooms here, but after what's happened between us, now I'm dying for more. There might be butterflies in my stomach, but there's also a smoldering just a little further down that's waiting for him to stir it up with his poker.

So to speak.

"So what was your plan for our date," I prod.

"Good question. To start, maybe watch for a while, get comfortable with the idea of participating, take it step by step, little by little." He laughs at my pout. "Until we're panting like animals and fucking up against one of the walls." His hand at my waist slides up towards my breast, stopping right beneath it.

Consider my smoldering core stoked.

I swallow deeply. "Um, listen."

"Too fast?"

With a confidence I wish I felt, I make sure there's no turning back. "No. I was going to say, can we skip over those first couple of steps, pretend that we did them and just move straight to the private room to work on the part with the panting?"

21

KEEGAN

Well, so much for taking it easy. Grinning down at the most beautiful woman in the entire club right after she just begged me to drag her off and have my way with her, I can't deny my jeans just got way tighter. What happened to the shy girl who came into my office a couple of weeks ago, terrified to give in to her urges?

That girl certainly wouldn't be wearing that sexy dress for me. It hugs Miranda's sleek curves so tightly, it's making me jealous of a damn piece of latex. I've wanted to peel it off since I first spotted her.

At this point, I'd love to buff my nails against my shirt and claim that her newfound bravery is all me, but at most, I triggered it. It was simmering under the surface the whole time, because no one changes this fast. Miranda was ready, she just needed a push in the right direction.

Talking with Gabe has made me feel a lot better about my feelings for Miranda. It helped to have someone else confirm that there probably is something different about her, and that difference is worth pursuing.

I hope.

But right now, we're here to have fun. Not over-think things "You sure you're ready to dive straight in?"

"I've been thinking about you—about this—without stop since I stayed at your place." She grips my forearm with both hands, her face a mask of determination. "Every time I've…" She swallows and blushes bright pink. Her lips pinch shut.

"You can't start like that and not finish. Every time you've what?"

Miranda's voice is so small I can barely hear it. "Every time I've… played with myself." She looks away, her face a veritable beacon in the dim lighting of the club. "I've been thinking of when you and I could… you know."

Immediately, my mind is flooded by images of her naked, on her bed, her fingers between her legs and her back arching as she comes. And she's been thinking about me while doing it. I nearly growl as I cradle her cheek in my hand and force her to look right at me. "You're going to show me."

Her eyes widen. "I'm… what?"

"Call me Sir."

She swallows nervously. "Yes… Sir."

"I'm going to take you to a private room, where you're going to take off that dress." I watch in pleasure as she nods, her lips parted and her eyes glazed with lust. "Then you're going to lie down, spread those sexy legs and you're going to play with yourself while I watch. I'm going to watch you make yourself come."

She doesn't answer, but licks her lips.

"Do you understand what I'll expect of you?"

With a nod, she replies softly, "Yes, Sir."

"And after you come, I'm going to make you come again, and again. I'm going to wear you out tonight." Seeing how her breasts rise and fall with her heavy breathing pushes me to grab her wrists and pin them down at the small of her back while pressing her against my chest. "Do you think you can handle that?"

"Yes, Sir." No hesitation, no nervousness. Just determination. I like that in my sub. And I love it in Miranda.

"Good." I flip her around so I'm still holding her wrists tightly in one hand, but now she's facing away from me. "Start walking." Amber sees me marching Miranda towards our room and waves. I nod back in acknowledgement, and then we're down the hallway with the private rooms.

Our room is the fifth one down. I stop Miranda in front, slide the key card I reserved earlier to unlock it and pull the door open. With the coast clear, I push her in ahead of me before locking the door behind us.

The rooms are pretty much the same, barring a couple of specialty areas, but we can save those for later. This is her first time playing without the guise of therapy and this room has everything we'll need tonight, and then some. A stocked rack of most any kind of whipping equipment you might imagine. A spanking bench, a St. Andrew's Cross, a leather couch—good for both play and aftercare—a shelf with toys, soy wax, everything. All of it shrink-wrapped and clean. Gabe is nothing if not professional.

But I don't need any of that, at least not yet.

Miranda's about to unzip her dress, but I raise my hand. "Wait. I'm going to undress you. Stand still until I tell you to move."

She starts, giving me a quick look before dropping her gaze. "Yes, Sir," she replies demurely. She lets her hands fall to her sides and waits for me.

I start by walking a slow circle around her, taking her sexy form in from every angle. The beautiful fall of her golden hair, the full curve of her breasts, the way her ass completes her hourglass figure in a way that makes me want to cover her fair skin with my marks. But there'll be time for that afterwards.

She doesn't turn her head, but she follows me with her eyes to the degree that she can. Her lips are just barely parted and she swallows often. I put my fingers gently against her throat, sliding the tips from just underneath her jaw to down into the hollow, where they bump against the top of her collar. Goosebumps pop up in their wake. Moving to her back, I lean in to place kisses on her exposed shoulder and up towards her neck.

Then I bite. Not hard, but enough to make her gasp.

It's time to open my present.

The zipper starts at her neck and runs almost all the way down her back. "Hands behind your head."

Quickly, she obeys, weaving her fingers together and putting them in place.

"Good," I encourage. Slowly, ever so slowly, I pull the zipper down. Her dress is clingy enough that it doesn't just fall, at least not until I touch my fingers to her waist through gap of the open zipper. I run them up along her sides, gently separating her from the dress, and when I reach forward to cup her full breasts, the dress falls to hang from her waist. She draws a sharp breath as I caress her soft flesh. Bending to kiss her neck, I murmur into her ear, "You have fantastic breasts."

"Thank you, Sir," she responds in a whisper.

I take my time, touching them, hefting them, capturing her hard nipples between my fingertips and rolling them. She closes her eyes, but is a good sub and doesn't move. She'll get her reward for that, but now I'm eager to see the rest.

Crouching, I hook my fingers by her waist and pull. The clingy material comes down, revealing a perfect heart-shaped ass, bisected by a lacy, black thong. As soon as I pull her dress past her hips, it no longer has anything to hang on to, and I let it drop.

What a vision, her in nothing but a thong, boots, gloves and that wonderful collar around her neck. It's only with great willpower that I stick to the plan. My dick is painfully cramped in my pants, and aching to be let out.

Soon.

"So fucking beautiful." Gripping her hips firmly, I hold her in place while I lean in to place a kiss on each of her ass cheeks. So pale and unblemished, a perfect canvas begging for the pink and red of a good spanking. Or the welted red stripes of a whip. Decisions, decisions.

"Tha—thank you, Sir." With a slight stutter, she can't hide that she's nervous, but she hasn't used her safewords.

Still. "Are you okay?"

"Yes, Sir. Thank you, Sir."

From behind, I can watch her sides expand and contract with her heavy breathing. I like that she's nervous. That she dares to step outside of her comfort zone. That she's willing to trust me.

As I tug her thong down, I can barely tear my eyes away, but I have to, at least for a moment. I consider what we have available to make my plan work. "How do you usually play with yourself?"

"What?" A short pause. "Sir?"

"On your back? On all fours? Chair, bed, floor?" The room is comfortably warm, intended for use while scantily dressed, or not at all. The floor is rubberized with a bit of give, but I want her up so I can see her better. The spanking bench could work, but the best bet might be the couch or the chair next to it.

"On my back, Sir, but there's no bed. Where do you want me?"

"In the chair, sweetness. Hook your legs over the arms, so I can see."

Wow, the blush does go all the way down, doesn't it?

But she obeys, if gingerly. Sitting carefully down in the chair with her legs demurely together, she delays as long as she can before she looks up to find me. No leniency here, I can promise her that. Not unless she uses a safeword. It must be obvious in my expression, because she doesn't argue.

That moment when she spreads her legs in front of me, opening herself up my gaze, to total vulnerability is the most breathtaking moment of sexiness I've ever experienced. I almost forget myself, spellbound by her naked beauty.

"I've… never let anyone see me do this before. I'm a little nervous." With a little smile, she fidgets with her hands, as if she doesn't know exactly where to begin.

"Start by closing your eyes. Pretend I'm not here," I suggest. She does. "What do you usually think about?"

She gives a short, embarrassed laugh. "You."

Basically what every guy ever wants to hear. I'm not going to last if I don't get her going.

"Okay, so pretend I'm watching you, thinking how beautiful you are. I'm rock hard, and I can't touch. All I can do is watch you be sexy."

Another laugh. "You *are* watching me."

"Yes, but this is fantasy me. The one who doesn't scare you or make you feel awkward, because he's not really here."

She nods, even if her expression doesn't look convinced. But she leans her head back to rest on the chair, and then slowly, tentatively, her right hand glides across her soft stomach to settle just above her glistening pussy. I love that she's still wearing her gloves. She might be nervous, but there's no doubt that she's turned on.

Moving closer, as quietly as I can, I kneel in front of her to watch. I'm so close that if she were to suddenly close her legs, she'd trap me between them.

22

MIRANDA

K eegan's right there. I can sense his gaze searing my skin everywhere his attention lands. I don't dare open my eyes, because if I do, I'll completely lose my nerve. Instead, I try to find that space in my mind where I usually find him, where I go when I have time alone to let my deepest fantasies unfold.

Without even really thinking about it, I touch myself, one hand spreading my own slickness over my clit while the other idly plays with my nipple. With the gloves on, it's almost like there's someone else touching me, but it feels nice.

Shivers chase each other across my skin while I move my fingers faster and faster. It's not long before I find just the right rhythm to bring me closer and closer to release. I pinch my nipple hard, then press two fingers into myself while rubbing my clit with my thumb, pretending that it's his teeth and cock stimulating me.

I'm not sure how long I play, but when I moan out loud, I'm barely aware that he's actually here and watching.

That is, until his tongue flicks past my hard-working fingers to touch my sensitive skin. I yelp in surprise and pull them away. They're immediately replaced by two of his, much thicker than my own. He closes his mouth around my clit and sucks.

Playing with myself is nice, but the real deal is so much nicer.

"Thank you, Sir," I groan as I flex my hips against him, pressing myself against his talented mouth.

"I couldn't fucking wait anymore. You looked so damned sexy like that. You'd better get used to playing with yourself while I'm around, because I can guarantee you I'm going to tell you to do it again."

God, he can tell me anything he likes if he's going to keep licking me like that. The combined assault of his rough, thrusting fingers and his broad tongue flitting into every sensitive crevice has me gripping the chair so I won't simply launch out of it.

He's so good. And he's mine.

Squeezing my eyes tightly shut, I arch my back as a tidal wave of dirty, sexy, sinful sensations washes over me. I'm so close, so incredibly close. With the arm rests for leverage under my legs, my ass isn't even touching the seat as I thrust myself at his mouth, willing him to bring me over the edge rather than keep me teetering on it.

And then he stops, pulling back with a glistening grin. I stare at him, nearly in a panic. "Nooo. Come back."

"You'd better watch your tone," he scolds with a raised finger, even though his eyes spark with amusement. "You've already earned some spanks. You wouldn't want me to tack on more, would you?"

"What, but I didn't—"

"Uh uh uh," he interrupts. "That's at least two more. You come when I say you come, not before."

Oh God, seriously? I was so so close, and I'm still tingling and shivering. It wouldn't take much to bring me back to the edge, either, but now I have to wait? "You're cruel."

His thick, dark brows furrow.

"Sir," I tack on in a rush, withering at the thought of his displeasure. If I piss him off, it'll take even longer.

"Stand up." He's tone is flat, yet commanding. It's the voice of a Dom who's displeased with his disobeying sub. The shivers down my spine are of a different kind this time, and I leap to my feet, nearly forgetting about the fact that I'm completely exposed to him.

"Yes, Sir. I'm sorry, Sir." I look up apologetically, and freeze for just a second. There's something familiar about the stern look on his face and the way he's holding his body. Shaking my head, I drive away the impulse to run and hide.

This is Keegan. I'm safe with him.

Keegan frowns, not angry, but concerned. "Are you all right?"

Swallowing nervously, I mentally force the memories that haunt my nightmares back into the deepest depths of my mind, where I can forget about them again. Then I nod. "Yeah, just a little nervous." I smile. "Sir."

A crooked smile curves his lips. "Okay. You know what to do if you're not."

"Yes, Sir."

He steps close, way inside my personal space. Placing a rough finger under my chin, he ensures that I can't look away. "While we're in here, I'm in charge. I expect no complaints, and no hesitation. Is that clear?"

I nod, letting Keegan's nearness fill my senses. "Yes, Sir."

"Barring safewords, of course."

"Yes, Sir."

"Good. Bring me those cuffs." He points at a selection of straps and buckles on the shelves by the door.

"Yes, Sir. How many?"

"Wrists and ankles."

"Yes, Sir." I hurry, happy to have a purpose.

When I return, he takes them from me without a word and goes to work on attaching them, one by one. He tightens each cuff carefully, ensuring with his little finger that they won't hurt my circulation, then he brings me to the cross attached to the wall. In rapid order, my cuffs are clipped to each point of the large X-shape so I'm facing the wall and my back is to him. He even finds a hook he can attach my collar to. I test my bonds, but all I get is a brief rattle of metal. There's no way I'm going anywhere.

He pats my ass, foreshadowing my punishment. "If you can't take orders, maybe a little discipline will impress the importance of obeying your master."

"Yes, Sir. I'm sorry, Sir." I'm just saying the same things over and over, but what else can I do?

He moves closer, pressing himself against my back, making me strikingly aware of the fact that while I'm basically naked, he's still fully dressed.

One of his hands slides up my side until it's cupping my breast, my nipple firmly held between his thumb and index finger. He squeezes until I draw a harsh breath between my teeth. The other hand goes to my hip and pulls me back against him. The cross is on a bit of a pedestal, so I'm at just the right level if he wants to take me right here. God, that would be sexy.

"I want to know that you're okay with this," he murmurs into my ear.

"I am, Sir." I just wish he wouldn't give me so much time to think about it.

"Normally I might not be so cautious, but we're still learning each other and communication is important."

"I'm fine, Sir. I trust you." And that's the scary truth. Somehow he's sneaked past my boundaries and I trust him to tie me up, to take care of me and to punish me. With Keegan, I know it'll be good for both of us. That's absolutely insane, isn't it? And yet, here I am, telling him that I'm okay with it.

Me

"And I trust *you* to be honest about this."

"Yes, Sir."

"Good." And with that, he smacks my ass firmly, leaving his hand there to grip it tight. "Because this is mine, and I intend to have my way with it."

I draw a sharp breath, and my earlier misgivings fall away. I'm right in the zone, right there with Keegan. His. "Yes, Sir."

"No point in waiting any longer, then." He takes a step back, and I know what's coming. My whole body tenses in anticipation. Fixing my gaze at the wall in front of me, I wait. "Ass out," he instructs.

Oh God. I've never been comfortable with posing sexy. I mean, I don't think I'm unattractive, but I'm not the type to flaunt anything either, even if it's for my lover. Swallowing a mixture of pride and embarrassment, I press my ass backwards, presenting it as a target.

Nothing happens.

I want so dearly to ask him to get on with it, but I don't even dare look over my shoulder. He's probably just waiting for me to do something else to punish me for, so I hold the position, back straight and ass out while trying to pretend I don't feel ridiculous.

"That is one sexy sight," he says appreciatively.

And then he spanks me, his hand impacting on my ass with a loud slap that echoes in the room. I shriek, caught off guard after his compliment. After all that anticipation, he still managed to nail me when I didn't expect it. Red tendrils of pain reach out from where he hit me, and instinctively, I arch away from him, pressing myself up against the cross.

"Back in position, sweetness." His tone makes it clear that if I'm not back there in no time flat, I'm getting more of the same. Well, even more. Why do I want this?

That spank hurt like crazy, and I suspect he was just warming up. I can stop everything right now if I want, but I already know I don't really want to. I might not understand why this calls to me, but I can't deny that it does. So instead of calling out a color, I push my ass back to where it was.

"Good." He spanks me again, the other cheek this time. You'd have thought a flogger would be more painful, but whether it's because my ass is bare, or he went easy on me before, his hand stings a lot worse. Even still, I don't flinch away this time. Once the initial shock wears off, I feel the invisible thread that connects us. Makes us two parts of a whole, each contributing an opposite half.

It makes me feel like I belong.

To him.

His hand connects again, forcing a sharp hiss from me. My ass is going to be bright red in the morning. It's the curse—or blessing, depending on who you ask—of having pale skin.

"I fucking love watching you take it. Your ass was made for this." I can hear the joy in his voice, and then the drawn breath as he swings again, hitting just where my ass meets my thigh. The sting surges right from where he connects with my sensitive skin, straight to between my legs. As he's getting warmed up, he's warming me up too. I adjust my legs a little for stability.

"Thank you, Sir."

Again he strikes, and this time he leaves his hand right there, like a burning brand until he slides it down past my asshole and finds my dripping folds.

I'd never imagined a spanking would get me this soaking wet, but maybe it has something to do with who's delivering it.

He pushes into me, making me moan and squeeze around his finger. "You seem to be enjoying yourself."

Has the air gotten thinner in here? I gasp. "Yes, Sir."

Starting slowly, he gets into an in-and-out rhythm that strokes me just the way I need. Maybe this time he'll actually let me come. He laughs, and I realize he won't, but there's nowhere for me to go. The little I can, I push back at him, hoping that if I'm quick, I can get there before he figures out what I'm doing.

No such luck.

With a sudden movement, he withdraws his finger and spanks me again. I cry out, more in surprise than from the pain. "You're greedy. I haven't given you permission yet." His voice is a heady mix of admonishment and amusement.

"Yes, Sir. I'm sorry, Sir."

God, I just want him to take me. Any way he wants, so long as he gets me there. My legs are shaking, and it's not from his strikes, but out of frustration, from desire, from the desperate need he's fueled in me.

He steps up right behind me again, growling into my ear while he reaches around to squeeze my breasts, "When we finally get there, you're going to be so desperate you'll do anything. I'll bring you right up to the edge, and when I'm ready— and only then—will I push you over. You'll never have come so hard in your life."

I press back, trying to grind myself against the front of his pants, against the hardness that I know is there, but he steps back with another laugh. "Greedy, greedy." Each word is accompanied by a smack on my ass. I moan deep in my throat in frustration.

"A dirty little girl like you is going to get exactly what she deserves"

Even as he says the words, my father's voice echoes in my head, saying almost the exact same thing, *You'd better behave, or I'll show you that bad little girls get what they deserve*. Suddenly, everything comes crashing down.

Dad's image flashes in front of me, the threat of his raised hand, the cruel sneer on his face. The cruelty that Mom faced for almost ten years, redirected towards me. Panic grips me, and I'm suddenly so very aware of how helpless I am, how vulnerable, how trapped.

This time, there's no way a few deep breaths can help. I'm completely unable to shake my panic.

"Red!" I scream, the room echoing the word back at me. "Red! Red!"

To Keegan's credit, he reacts with the speed of lightning. In moments, he has my cuffs released. He tries to take me in his arms. "Miranda, what's wrong. What's going—"

I push away. "Don't touch me!"

He looks dumbstruck at my tone. Shit, it wasn't supposed to go like this. It's not really his fault, but the way my mind is whirring, I can't help myself.

"I'm sorry, just please. Don't touch me. I can't—"

Shit.

23

MIRANDA

"Miranda, what can I do? Please, talk to me. Let me help." Keegan's voice is strained. He's obviously holding himself back with a lot of effort.

"I'm sorry, I need to go." My dress and panties are still on the floor where he dropped them. I rush over to pull them on, growling in frustration when the waistband catches on one of my heels.

"What? Please. Something obviously triggered you. We should talk about it." Concern is written all over his face, but my mind is going haywire. I hate that Dad has this kind of hold on me so many years later, but I'm too upset to talk right now. Not when all I can see is my father standing over me with his hand raised.

"I can't. No. Not yet. I'm sorry." Words pour out of me as I struggle with my zipper. It was difficult enough when I put it on the first time, but now that I'm so off kilter, it's nearly impossible.

"Can I at least help you with that? I won't touch you. Just pull the zipper up. Then we can talk about this later, if that's what you need."

I make one more frustrated try, but lose my grip on the little metal tab. Burying my face in my hands, I try to stand as still as I can, though I'm shaking like a leaf. Then I nod. "Okay, just… just don't touch."

"Okay. Okay, I'll try. I'm coming up behind you, really slowly okay? I'm not going to make any sudden moves. Just your zipper."

For a moment, I think this is going to work. Maybe I can even calm down a little so we can figure it out. He just has to get the—

"No, keep away." I leap forward out of his reach at the first sensation of his hand near my back. "I can't. I'm sorry. I need to get out."

He stares at me, obviously frustrated by his help-lessness.

Holding my dress up with one hand, I use the other to push the door open. Keegan starts as if he's going to follow, but holds himself back. "At least tell me where you're going. You shouldn't be alone right now."

I shake my head. Everything is wrong. My chest aches, and my cheeks are wet with tears. "I can't…" I push the door back with my ass, keeping myself facing him.

"Are you going home? Let me order you a car and I'll follow to make sure you get there safely. I'll keep my distance."

He's doing and saying all the right things. Why is this happening to me now, of all times? I thought I'd shaken my childhood off, but Dad's still the devil riding on my shoulder.

"Please. I need space. Please." Now that I'm out in the hall, people are looking, and I hate their curious stares and the suspicious glances they're sending Keegan. I look at the closest ones, a couple in leather outfits. "It's not him. It's me. He's not doing anything wrong, I swear."

"Miranda," Keegan calls from the doorway. As much as it must pain him, he hasn't moved. He lifts his hand towards me, but as a look of sadness passes over him, he lets it drop again. "I just want to help."

The door to one of the private rooms pops open, and Amber peeks out, followed by Eric. "Miranda! What's wrong?" She's only half dressed, but she rushes over to me anyway and envelops me in a bear hug. I flinch at her touch, but relax quickly. Amber, at least, I can handle. She looks up at Keegan. "If you've hurt her, I swear to God I'm going to tear off your head and stuff it up your ass!"

I pat at her, trying to get her attention. "It's okay. Please. It's not his fault, I promise."

Keegan approaches Eric with a serious look on his face. "I need you to help make sure she gets somewhere safe, home or wherever she asks."

Eric frowns and narrow his eyes. "Is there a reason she can't trust you to do that?"

"Please," Keegan asks, hands raised. "She had a bad reaction to something during our scene and right now, I'm a reminder of whatever that is."

Intense embarrassment, no, utter humiliation, settles down over me like a big, ugly blanket that Amber's friendly arms can't keep away. "He didn't do anything wrong, honest. I'm the one that's broken." The look on Keegan's face at my words just makes me feel guiltier.

Eric makes a quick trip into their room to get the rest of Amber's clothes. She takes them gratefully and tugs them on in a hurry while he glares at the onlookers who suddenly realize they have other places to be. "I'll go get the car and meet you up front."

My heartbeat flutters unhappily. "Um, is it okay if just Amber drives?"

"What? Why?" Eric takes a step back, confused.

"I just… I just want to go home," I say in a small, sad voice. I'm ruining everyone's night and it's all my fault.

Something in my tone seems to get through, and he nods. "Whatever you need, alright? I'll take a cab back to our place later. You and Amber take all the time you need." He directs another pointed glance in Keegan's direction.

Not that Keegan sees it, because he's totally focused on me. "I'll give you an hour, then I'm sending a text if I don't hear from you. You don't need to talk to me if you don't want, but let me know you all right either yourself, or have Amber do it."

"I'll make sure she's okay," Amber announces, shrugging into her short leather jacket. "Let's get you out of here, babe." She takes my arm and pulls me along, dragging me past more gawking faces. I don't even care if they look, so long as I don't have to stay.

Two minutes later, Amber and I are outside and I take a deep breath. The air is cool tonight, but inside it felt like my lungs were too small, and now I can finally start to relax. I know if I turned around, I'd see Keegan and probably Eric at the doors, but I can't bring myself to make that connection, not yet.

Amber slips her arm around my waist and leads me down the street towards the parking lot. She doesn't say anything until she's got me in the car and is pulling out. "So what happened in there? You freaked out."

I shake my head before I drop it into my hands. "It's nothing."

"Like hell it is." She gives me a withering look.

"Watch the road." I point.

She returns her attention to the windshield, but that doesn't keep her from talking. "You went ballistic. I heard you through the door. That's not the quiet wallflower that I've gotten to know." She sighs. "God, you've got me on edge now too. But if Keegan has done anything to you that you didn't want him to—"

"He didn't. Please. You all think it's him, but it's me. I'm the one who went all crazy, and now I've embarrassed him, and maybe even gotten him in trouble. I don't know how to fix this, but I've messed up."

"A reaction like that isn't messing up. That's something happening. Something significant. What you need right now is support, good friends and comfort. Is your mom still at your place?" I nod, though Amber must see the grimace that accompanies it. "Do you want to crash at our house tonight? We can talk, I'll make hot cocoa, and I'll tell Eric to take a hike for the evening. If he calls

Paul or Gabe, I'm sure either of them would be happy to let him crash on the couch for the night."

Amber is a sweetheart, but just because I'm a basket case, doesn't mean I can intrude like that. "No, I couldn't chase Eric out of his own home. Just drive me——"

"It's decided then. I'll call him once we get there. And you can call you mom and let her know, so she doesn't get worried."

"Amber." For the first time since I freaked, I feel a little smile coming. "Honestly, you can take me home. I need to talk to Mom anyway."

"And you will, after we've had a girls' night in. I'll find something sappy or funny on Netflix and we'll huddle up under blankets and drink hot chocolate. Or something stronger, if you prefer that. And then we'll talk, if you want."

I give up. What Amber wants, Amber gets.

She pulls into their garage and phones up Eric while I call Mom who seems relieved that I'm with a girlfriend. After that, we do exactly what she said, and while La La Land plays on the TV, I tell her the whole story. It's cathartic, but the whole time, I wonder how Keegan is doing and where he is. When my phone beeps, I'm not ready to talk to him yet, and without saying a word, Amber picks hers up and sends a quick text. By the time the whole mess starts to feel far enough off that I'd consider looking at my messages, we're both so tired that we pass out in her living room.

24

MIRANDA

"Hello? Anybody home?" I shut the front door to my apartment behind me. It's almost noon, but Amber refused to let me leave before she'd made me breakfast. Eric had already called, asking if it was okay for him to come home yet, and I was feeling bad enough for him getting booted out as it was. Amber is wonderful, but she does what she wants, when she wants, that's for sure.

"Miranda!" Mom appears from the living room. She smiles, but her face looks drawn. "You're back. Are you okay? You sounded... off on the phone last night. And this sudden sleepover. I've hardly slept, worrying about you."

She opens her arms, and I hug her back. Yeah, she drives me nutty, but she's my mom, and what happened last night reminded me of something. We're survivors together.

"I'm going to make myself a hot chocolate, and then I want to talk. Is that okay? Do you want anything?"

"Of course that's okay. Don't worry about me. I've still got a half-full mug of tea."

A few minutes later, I drop into the couch opposite hers after putting my mug on the coffee table. "So…"

Mom puts down her knitting magazine with a frown and searches my face for clues. "What's going on with you? Is it Keegan?"

"No. Well, yes." I shake my head. "Sort of."

"Well, now that you've cleared that up…"

I lean back, blowing hair out of my face in frustration. How do I even begin to explain? How much needs explaining? "Dad ruined my date."

Mom's eyes go wide at that. Her voice shakes when she asks, "Your father? He's not—"

"Oh God, no. He's not here. I haven't spoken to him since… well, since before we ran. That's not what I meant. When I was out with Keegan, we got in… a situation, where I suddenly got a flash-back from… from back then." I drop my hands to my lap and squeeze them nervously between my thighs. I feel like a little girl again, helpless.

Mom gets up, comes around the coffee table and sits next to me before wrapping me up in a big hug. "Oh, baby girl. This is why I finally ran. I just wish I'd done so earlier. Or that I'd never met him in the first place."

I cling to her in a way I haven't done since I was little. I rest my head on her shoulder and close my eyes. "No, I'm glad you met him. Otherwise I wouldn't be me, and I wouldn't have you. I just wish he wasn't… well, you know."

She nods. "You are the only part of that relation-ship that wasn't a mistake. If I had to go through it all over again just to get you, I would."

"Well, I'm here, so you won't have to." I tighten my hug with a smile.

After a few minutes of cuddling, Mom pats my back. "So what happened? I'm a little afraid to ask what Keegan might've done to bring this on, but you know I'm here for you, no matter what."

"It was... I don't know how to explain this."

"Try me."

Nope, there's no way I'm telling Mom about kinky play at a BDSM club. "He didn't do anything wrong. I swear. It was just something about the way he moved, or something he said that pulled me right back to life with Dad. He couldn't have known it'd trigger the response it did."

Mom strokes my hair, and it's really soothing. "What kind of response?"

"I heard Dad threaten me. Clear as day. And then it was like, I knew Keegan wasn't Dad, but he was a man, you know? I totally freaked out." I nuzzle closer.

"Did he hit you?"

My head snaps up at that, and I stare at her. "What? No!" I mean, technically, he did, but not like how she means.

She holds my gaze, her expression tight, searching for the lie. I'm the first to look away. "Honey, I lived it. You know that. You can't hide these things from me."

"He didn't. Not really. Not like you're thinking."

"Miranda."

I push off, and this time I meet her gaze again without fear. "It was an… intimate thing, okay? I'll swear on whatever you want that it was totally consensual."

Her cheeks turn red. "Intimate?"

I'd like topics I'd never want to discuss with my mother for a thousand dollars, please, Alex. "Do we have to talk about this? I'm not really comfortable with it."

Mom takes a deep breath and winces slightly as she speaks, "Was it like… *spanking?*" The word comes out in a strained whisper.

Oh God. "Mom!"

"I might be over the hill and about as boring as they come, but I'm not completely square. Your generation didn't invent sex, Miranda. And as your grandmother reminded me occasionally, neither did mine." She looks vaguely green, but determined.

"Okay, look. Yes, it was… something like that." I take a sip of my cocoa, only to find it almost all the way cooled. It's still sweet and creamy, though, and it gives me a moment to gather my thoughts. "It was something I wanted to explore, but maybe… maybe I wasn't really ready, and know Keegan probably thinks I'm a flake."

No, he knows I'm a flake. He's my therapist after all.

"Honey, if he loves you, he'll love you, flakes and all, but you're going to have to help me understand this."

"This?"

Mom picks up her knitting and puts it back down again nervously. "Why would you want something like *that?* After everything we've been through."

Where do I even begin with this? "It's hard to explain."

"Not too much detail, please."

At least that we agree on. "Yeah, of course. I think... I think I wanted to find a way to take back what Dad stole."

"How on earth could *that* help anything?" Mom looks both confused and horrified. "I'm sorry, but hitting is abuse."

"It's not hitting. It's just another way to spice things up, like wearing something sexy, or... I don't know, saying naughty things." I cringe internally at how lame I sound, but come on, I'm talking to my *mom*. About S. E. X. Kinky sex.

She looks just as uncomfortable as I feel, but she hasn't run away or called the police yet so it could be worse. "I think that's about as much detail as I want about that, but I still don't understand why you thought it would help you."

I've thought about this a lot, and Keegan and I talked about it in our sessions, before things got complicated. "Growing up with Dad the way he was, there was always the fear of violence hanging over us. Even before he finally hit me, there were so many times where I knew, I *knew*, he hit you, and I could see in his eyes that one day it would be my turn." Mom's eyes glisten with unshed tears, and she nods. "As I got older, I don't know, maybe it was something I'd always be interested in, or maybe not, but I started to feel like this, um, spicy stuff, could help me not be so afraid. Because this time it would be my choice."

"Oh, honey. I'm not sure I'll ever really understand."

"I know. That's okay. Trust me, if it were up to me we wouldn't be having this conversation, but as much as I love Amber, I need to talk to someone who was there." I look right at Mom. "Someone who understands what we went through."

She grabs my hand and squeezes. For several long moments, we sit there in silence, not knowing what to say.

"You should come home with me."

I sigh and shake my head. "I can't hide away from this. I've been hiding my whole life, and I only just dared to face it head on. I really like this guy, Mom." Maybe even love him. "And I'm afraid if I back away now, I'll never get the courage to try again."

"You're still young. There's no need to push. You have plenty of time to——""

"What if he's the one? What if he's the one and I let my fear of a man who doesn't deserve the time of day scare me away from finding out?"

The next time she speaks, her voice is small. "I can't protect you if you stay here. There's been too much hurt in your life already."

Says my mom, who's been hurt more than anyone I know. I have to swallow before I choke up. "I know, but… but sometimes we have to face these things. And it makes us stronger. Think about you now, compared to before you dared break away from him. You're the strongest person I know, Mom."

"Being strong is painful sometimes." She sighs. "But if this is what you really want, you know I'll always be there for you even if I don't understand your choices."

I bite my lip, thinking immediately of how pain and strength can go hand in hand in a positive way too. Is that what went wrong? I'm just not strong enough? I can't believe that. I refuse to believe that, but it's something I should talk with Keegan about.

God, if he even wants to see me again. After the way I ran out, leaving him there like he was some kind of criminal. I haven't even had the courage to check my phone, though I know Amber let him know I was all right.

All right.

I'm so far from that it's crazy.

"What I want…" I trail off. What do I want? "I want to be able to do what I want, without being afraid of Dad's memory haunting me while I do it. And I'm not going to be able to do that back home."

"Well, obviously I can't convince you." She sighs, then smiles faintly. "I have to try. Maybe I could move in here?" Mom laughs at the look on my face after she suggests us being roomies. "Kidding. I'd stay if you needed me, but this place isn't for me. I've lived my life, baby. I might not be ready for the home yet, but I'm not like you, young and with my whole future ahead of me."

"You know I love you, right?"

Mom hugs me tight. "I know. I know better than anyone how big your heart is, which is why as charming as he was when we met, I'm not sure how I feel about this Keegan anymore. Are you sure he deserves you?"

"I am."

"I thought that about your father once."

"Sometimes trust is broken." I sigh. "I realize that. I'm not stupid. Sometimes we trust the wrong people. But if we never trust again, is that any better? You've been alone for so long. Are you happy?"

"How can you ask that? I have you."

There are tears in both our eyes, but we're smiling too. "It's not the same. I worry about you too, you know."

There's a sadness in her face I wish I could wipe away, but there's only so much I can do. Some burdens can be shared, but others we need to figure out on our own when we're ready. She nods, slowly. "Maybe one day. Mr. Broswell has been slipping extra sausages in my bag lately. You never know."

I pray to God that's not a euphemism. "Mr. Broswell? The butcher? His wife just died!"

Mom raises an eyebrow. "Three years ago, dear. This is why you should come home occasionally."

I'm starting to understand why Mom didn't want details, but the tension between us is gone, replaced by something fragile, but more real than we've had in a long time.

It's not perfect, but it's a start, and if I can have a conversation like this with my mother, it gives me hope that maybe I haven't permanently screwed everything up with Keegan.

25

MIRANDA

Can I call you?

Keegan's text drops in with a loud pling that startles me enough that I almost drop my phone. And here I was, trying to formulate a message to him that sounds more meaningful and less whiny than "Please don't hate me."

God, I'm still so embarrassed about last night. And how must he feel? Left behind and looking like the bad guy. I hope he didn't get in trouble at the club. Even in my state, I couldn't miss some of the ugly glares people were sending his way. I owe him big time.

So instead of texting back, I grab the bull by the horns and call him.

"Miranda," he answers. "How are you doing?"

How am I doing? I take stock, feeling myself out. "I'm okay, I think. Still a little rattled after yesterday, but a lot better."

"I'm sorry."

"I'm sorry."

We blurt the words out at the same time, but after a shared awkward laugh, I'm the first to keep going. "You have nothing to be sorry about, Keegan. You only did what I asked you to. I'm sorry for messing it all up. I made you look terrible. Did you get in trouble?"

"Nothing that I couldn't handle. I had a chat with Gabe after, and Eric confirmed my story. I'm sure he'd like to speak with you, too, but no rush. The person I'm worried about is you. I shouldn't have let you get in so deep. You weren't ready, and I should've seen that."

"I *was* ready. At least I thought I was. You were amazing."

He snorts. "Sure. Amazingly good at ignoring the obvious. Miranda, I was terrified that I'd broken you. Hell, I fucked up."

I shake my head, even if he can't see it. "No, you didn't do anything wrong. I just wasn't as ready as I thought. We'll try again—I mean, if you still want to. Please still want to."

"You have no idea how much I want to, and that's the problem."

"What? No, that's not a problem. We'll just be careful. We can go slower. It wasn't your fault. It was Dad's."

"Your father's?"

"Yeah, I… well, with all of this thinking about the past, the old bastard's been cropping up a lot in my mind lately. Even in my nightmares, and I haven't had those since I was younger. They're scary, but… well, I didn't think they'd affect me like that."

His sigh comes clearly through the phone. "You should've told me about this. Especially given your therapy."

"I'm telling you now. I swear, I'll tell you everything. Don't give up on me." I bite my lip and wait for his reply.

"I'll never give up on you, and that's why I have to do this." He draws a deep breath. "I should've seen it coming, but I've been blinded by how crazy I am about you. I pushed you too quickly, and I let you run the show when I'm the one who's supposed to know what he's doing. I failed you, Miranda."

Oh no. My stomach drops at his words. It's not so much what he's saying as what he's not saying that's beginning to sink in.

"I guess, in the back of my mind, I've known for a while," he continues. "I just haven't wanted to admit it. But what happened last night, it showed me just how far wrong I'd let things go."

I blink, my eyes stinging. "That doesn't mean we can't fix it. We'll go slower. I'll do everything you say. Just the way you tell me to."

"We can't. This is why there are laws about this, why I should never have agreed to be your therapist after that first session, and definitely not after we kissed. You're amazing, Miranda, but you're my patient, and I can't get you out of my mind. That immediately should've disqualified me from helping you, much as I hate to say it."

I quell the panic attack building in the back of my head. "Okay. Okay, that's bad, but we can figure this out. Sure. We just have to sit down, talk it through and see what our options are. We can fix this." And here I thought things were heading in the right direction after my talk with Mom. You'd think trying to get her over on my side would be the most challenging thing for me to do today.

"I can't. I'm hurting you."

"You're helping me!"

"I've got some recommendations for other therapists I know who have experience with the kinkier side of things. They'll be objective enough to get you the help you really need." He sounds resigned and sad, like he's reading a eulogy.

"No! I want you!" Wetness slides down my cheeks and I'm sure Mom can hear me from her room, but I don't care. "You're the man who finally managed to pry me out of my shell, and now that I'm finally becoming who I want to be, you're pulling out? You can't do this."

"Miranda!" His voice turns stern, his Dom voice. I shut up immediately. "I have to do this. I need you to get better, and I am so fucking blinded by my love for you, and my desire to be with you, that I can't ensure that you do. I know you're hurting, and probably angry at me right now for saying it, but buried under all of that, you'll find that much as I hate it, I have to do the right thing. And the right thing for both of us is for me to let you go. You need someone who isn't blinded by their feelings." He sighs. "Just by caring for you, even if that was all it was, I'd be risking your health. I can't be responsible for that, and I shouldn't be. I'm sorry."

"Okay. Fine." My voice quavers, much as I try to keep it steady. My lips are tightly pursed, because if I don't force them into place, I'm going to lose it. "So if I see a different therapist, then we can be together, right? Because then you're no longer my therapist, and I'm no longer your patient."

"It's not that easy."

"It *is* that easy!"

"It's not. I've explained this to you before. I'll just look like I've been grooming you. By law, we should wait at least two years."

"I don't care. Who's going to know?"

"That's part of the problem. You *should* care. You should have the perspective to understand why we need some time apart. I might not mean to be, but I'm a bad influence on you. I do the wrong things just because I care too much. It may seem right, but I'm telling you, I'm bad for your progress. That's not going to change just because you're not coming to me for therapy anymore. The damage is already done."

"This isn't fair, Keegan." I sniffle, and not too delicately. There's a silent pause on the other end of the line.

"Listen, Miranda. You've found yourself, or at least started down that path. If I've done anything right, it's to help you find direction, but I'm not the right guide for you. I can't be, not with the way I feel."

"How can you possibly claim to love me, when all you're going to do is leave?"

"Don't you get it?" His frustration carries clearly through the line. "That's exactly why I have to leave. Because I love you. Nothing we have can be real until you have the distance and help you need, and it's very likely that you won't want me by the time that happens. You deserve better."

"I deserve you, but I'm starting to wonder if you deserve me!"

"You're right. I don't. I fucked this up from the start, and now I'm cutting it off before things get any worse. I'm sorry, Miranda. I truly am. I'll always love you."

"That's it? You'll always love me, but from afar?" Anger drives my words. "Good thing you're leaving now then, before I get really attached. You… you…" A whole slew of bad names flash through my mind, but I can't quite bring myself to say any of them.

"I can only say I'm sorry so many times. But I am." His voice sounds pained and tired. "I'll send you an email with some recommendations, okay? People who I know are good at what they do, and can be trusted to be professional. They'll take care of you, if you'll let them. Goodbye, Miranda."

"Fuck you, Keegan," I seethe into the phone, and then it goes dead. That doesn't keep me from yelling at it, "And if you're such a good therapist, maybe you should take a look at yourself and your goddamn martyr complex." Then I throw the phone with a clatter onto my nightstand and throw myself angrily on my bed.

"You stupid idiot," I mumble while tears crawl down my cheeks.

There's a cautious knock on the door. "Miranda? Are you all right?"

No. "Yeah, Mom, I'll be okay." Eventually. Probably.

"I'm coming in," she warns, and when I don't deny her, she does. Sitting herself down next to me, she takes my head and cradles it against her chest as she embraces me. "I think I overheard enough to get the general gist of what happened. I wasn't listening, mind you, but you weren't exactly quiet."

I nod into her tear-soaked shirt. I hadn't been exactly subtle. "He doesn't want me anymore. You were right. Men can't be trusted."

"Shh, not now." And then she rocks me like she used to when I was little. It's comforting, but it doesn't fill the big, black hole that Keegan just punched into my chest, right where my heart used to be.

26

KEEGAN

Well, fuck, that might be the hardest thing I've ever had to do.

Shit.

Fuck.

Goddamn it.

Motherfucker.

But it was the right thing to do. I'm going to keep telling myself that until I believe it.

Tossing my phone on my bed, I get up to look out the window. Three floors down, the city moves in its regular patterns, oblivious to my world coming apart up here. Cars come and go, people walk past, everything seems so fucking perfectly normal out there. With a growl, I stomp out of the bedroom to go make myself a coffee.

I pace the kitchen while the machine, identical to the one at the office, grinds the beans and heats the water. I'm like a lion in a cage, refusing to leave even though the door's wide open.

I did the right thing. Better to cut the rope now and drift away. She'll get better, stronger, and find someone else.

Fuck, that cuts too deep to think about.

Outside, the wind's kicked up and dark clouds are coming in quickly. It's going to be stormy tonight, which feels very appropriate. Something to accompany my dark mood. Out on one of the balconies, something blows around in the wind and bangs against the outside wall.

I was expecting to feel some kind of relief after talking to Miranda, but all I feel is numb. It's very tempting to spend the day getting flat-out drunk and put this out of my mind, but then what? I'm supposedly good at counseling others, as long as they're not Miranda, so why is it so hard to counsel myself?

Returning to my bedroom, I set my coffee on the nightstand and drop back onto my bed. I should do something today to get my mind off this. Get out a little or something.

My phone's blinking at me. Probably nothing good, but trained by years of keeping my phone notifications at bay, I pick it up to check. Email. I should know better than checking, right? But I do.

From Miranda.

Hi Keegan,

You're probably not even reading this, but I had to write something. You're making a huge mistake. I hope you realize that, but you're probably still proud of yourself for how you're doing the right thing and how this is best for me. *insert bossy masculine voice here*

I'll admit I chuckle a little. In my mind I can picture her putting on a gruff voice and imitating me, right before I give her a solid spank for her impertinence. Fuck, I'm going to miss her.

Mom said I shouldn't try to talk to you yet, or ever, and that I'm better off putting you behind me, so I guess you two have finally found something you agree on. I told her to mind her own business, so now she's glowering at me from the couch as I write this. You'd better appreciate what I'm going through here.

That ease of mind I was looking for earlier comes seeping in, at least just a little, while I read Miranda's words. If our situation wasn't so fucked up, it might almost be enjoyable. She doesn't understand that I'm doing this for both of us. I couldn't live with myself if she looked at me one day with doubt in her eyes.

I'm rambling, I guess. You're probably used to it. Anyway, you never let me say goodbye. If you're really set on this, and planning to remove yourself completely from my life, then I want you to know that no matter how it ended, what you did for me can't ever be expressed fully in words. I could only show you, and now you're going away so I can't even do that. And that hurts. It really hurts. I'm really mad at you right now, but I still don't want you to go.

Please, rethink this. We can figure it out together. Maybe I'll get hurt doing it, but I think what we have is worth fighting for.

At least I did.

If you really don't think we do, then there's nothing I can do about it by myself. And I'll probably think you're a jerk for the rest of my life. So you'll have to live with that.

I love you (jerk or not).

Miranda

Well, fuck. I lay back on the sheets, scrubbing at my eyes with the palms of my hands. Never mind feeling better. Now I feel even more like an ass than I did before.

I didn't even think that was possible, but it doesn't change anything.

She needs space to figure herself out, and so long as I'm there, she'll use our feelings as a crutch to ignore what's really going on inside her brain. I wish there was another way, because this hurts like hell and she'll probably end up hating me.

I could try to still see her occasionally, but I don't trust either of us to do that right now without making another mess.

Should I write her back? What would be the point?

Goddamnit!

No matter what I do it feels wrong.

I did the right thing!

Wish it felt that way.

27

MIRANDA

I wrap my shawl closer around my shoulders. It was cooler tonight than I planned for, and even within the club, I'm not quite thawed enough to let that one flimsy layer go. I don't know exactly what I expect to do here, but after three months of cautious counseling after the Keegan debacle, I couldn't put it off anymore.

He did as promised and sent me a list of therapists. All women, of course. It took a few days of angry sulking, but I did eventually start calling them. Apparently, he'd contacted each one in advance to let them know I might call. Not sharing any details, but asking them to consider me as a new client. After a few conversations, I even found one I liked, though I miss the excitement of my sessions with Keegan.

After three months of working with Doctor Wendy, I definitely feel better. I haven't dreamed about Dad in over a month, and at her recommendation, I took a break from the club. It's frustrated Amber to no end, but it's given me the opportunity to reframe what I want, both from BDSM and the rest of my life.

Even though I hated him for what he did, Keegan was looking out for me in his own way. He never replied to my email, but he got me the best help he could. In some ways I wish I still hated him, because there's this giant hole in my heart that aches for him every day. But as Amber has told me several times over, it's his loss.

One day I might even believe her.

Why am I here, again? I'm in no mood to dance, but find myself pressing into the gyrating crowd anyway, just to warm up. It works. Once I'm surrounded by sweat-slicked bodies with energy to spare, it's not long before I'm wearing my shawl like a sash and wishing I could strip further to stay cool. A topless woman languidly squeezes by while dancing with a shirtless man in black jeans. For a second, I consider following their lead, but only a second, I'm not quite there yet.

Besides, without Keegan, what's the point? Showing myself off to strangers isn't my thing. In theory, Keegan isn't my thing either, not anymore. That doesn't mean I'm putting myself on display for anyone else yet, though.

Somewhere in this mob, Amber's waiting for me. After three months off, that familiar itch to be here came back and when I took it up with Wendy, she surprisingly agreed, so long as I promised to go easy. I've come a long way in her care, and although our sessions have been more talk than action, she cleared me to give it a cautious go.

I have to call her in the morning to let her know how it goes, though. Scanning the room, I don't think there'll be much to report. As much fun as people seem to be having, Keegan's still too fresh in my mind.

A large man I've never seen before dances my way, moving sinuously in time to the heavy beats of the music. His crisp white button-down shirt is open to display an undeniably impressive chest, and the rolled-up sleeves reveal a pair of powerful forearms. He's definitely got the physique down. The shirt's haphazardly tucked into a well-fitting pair of ripped jeans, giving him a classy bad boy combo look that's surprisingly sexy.

It would look even better on Keegan.

No, I'm not supposed to be thinking about him tonight.

I force myself to look up to actually see the guy's face, and it's nice. He's got a sexy smile, and deep blue eyes under an intentionally untidy shock of brown hair. In fact, if I weren't still coming down from the guy I thought might be the one, he'd be the kind of guy I'd happily check out.

But I am, so even as the guy is coming closer, I smile and shake my head, a gesture I had plenty of practice with in the days before I met Keegan. I'm not looking for a dance partner tonight. Or any kind of partner. His smile doesn't falter, but he shrugs in a too bad sort of gesture, then starts scanning for someone more receptive.

Maybe once I've had a bit more time, I'll consider actually meeting some new people here. It'd make Amber happy, at least.

Pressing past the dancing crowd, now more than happy to find a cooler part of the club, I arrive at the corridor into the play area. The gateway to sin, one might say. Amber suggested that tonight was good, so maybe there's a good show going on. I haven't been keeping up with the postings since all this began. I have no idea what's going on anymore.

As usual, the area is crowded with excited players, in all shapes, sizes and colors. One of the things that always attracted me to this club was the enthusiastic acceptance of diversity. Your kink's not my kink isn't a disparaging remark here, just a way to say that we're into different things, and that's okay. So if you like to be tickled senseless, like the tall man strapped to the cross in the corner, and according to the sign next to him, available to anyone who wants, then that's okay, even if the idea of it gives me the heebie jeebies. Or maybe the face sitting that those two women are doing, or the full-body rubber suits, or whatever. In this place, I'm nearly bordering on vanilla, but I don't begrudge them their fun.

I wait for that little kinky tingle inside to kindle, but without Keegan, nothing looks interesting. Maybe I'm not really ready.

Maybe I never will be.

Turning around, I take a step, only to bump right into a brick wall of tall, masculine chest. Sense would say that he'd at least get knocked a little bit off balance, but it's me who bounces back.

"I'm sorry," I get out while catching my balance.

Strong hands grab my shoulders to steady me. "No, I'm sorry, I wasn't looking where I was—"

I recognize the voice long before his words cut off in surprise.

When I look up, Keegan's staring down at me. He's looking good tonight. Tight charcoal gray T-shirt that's stretched across his chest. Dark jeans cradle his ass in a way that's impossible not to notice, held in place by a wide leather belt. His hair's mussed in a way that automatically makes me think of sex, though to be fair, it's difficult to look at him and not think of sex.

At first I'm at a loss for words, but then I find some and they're not very nice. "How dare you?"

He blinks, then frowns as his face closes down. "What do you mean, how dare I?"

"You dumped me, and now you're back at my club? It was so important to separate yourself from me, but then here you are, as if nothing ever happened. Did you even think about how that would make me feel? Jerk." A part of me insists that maybe I'm being a little unreasonable, but I can't quite hold it back either. I'm still mad at him, and I'd sort of assumed that I'd gotten the club in our breakup.

People around us turn to watch curiously. The tall shaved-head guy who's usually watching the door happens to be nearby, and takes a step closer. "Everything all right here?" He glances at my opponent. "Keegan?"

They would know each other.

Keegan puts his hand up. "It's okay, Caleb. Nothing to worry about."

When Caleb looks at me questioningly, I nod back. "We're fine." He backs up, but keeps an eye on us, ready to step in if things get heated.

"Come on," Keegan says, taking my wrist and walking towards the private rooms.

I rip my hand out of his grip. "Don't touch me," I hiss, trying to keep the volume down.

"Dammit, do you really want to do this here? I was just thinking that we could discuss this away from the fucking peanut gallery."

For a moment, I glance back at Caleb, who's standing there with his bulging arms crossed over his broad chest, watching the crowd in general, but throwing constant glances in our direction.

"Fine." I might not trust Keegan to not break my heart, but I do trust him not to hurt me, unless I ask him to. And not even then, now. "Let's go."

His shoulders relax with relief. "Great. Here."

The room he leads me to is similar to the other ones we used. Slightly different furniture in slightly different places. The spanking bench is further to the side and there's no cross, but there's a tall king size bed instead, with barred head and footboards, perfect for attaching cuffs or ropes to.

But I'm not here to play, so it really doesn't matter what the furnishings are. As soon as he closes the door behind us I whirl on him. "What the hell are you doing here?"

"What do you mean? Amber specifically told me to be here tonight." He looks genuinely confused.

Amber... Oh, I'm going to have a chat with that girl later.

"Well, then maybe she's the one you should be talking to."

"Fuck, I knew this was a bad idea." He looks frustrated, but still so handsome it kills me not to reach out and touch him. "I thought you knew I was coming. If you're not ready, I'll go." His brilliant green eyes stare at me intently. "I would never have come if I knew it would make you unhappy, Miranda. Have a good night."

Keegan turns to leave, tearing the hole in my heart wider by the step.

"Wait."

He stops, hand on the door.

"I… I have to know. Have you missed me? At all?" my voice cracks on the last question.

"Have I—" He chokes out a bitter laugh. "Not a second has gone by where I didn't question what I did. All of it, but even if it makes me a bastard, I can't find it in myself to regret meeting you." Keegan turns, his expression so raw it should bleed. "I didn't walk away because I didn't care, I walked away because I cared too much. Three months won't change that. I'm not sure three lifetimes would. This was about you, not me."

"Bullshit," I spit.

"Excuse me?"

I ignore his angering tone, barreling on. "Ending our professional relationship was for the best. I know that now, but not answering my email? Pulling away from me like I meant nothing and not even sending an occasional snooty text to see how I was doing? That's just because you were too chickenshit to find out if I'd changed my mind about you."

"Jesus Christ, that's not how it is. I've checked up with Amber and talked with Wendy. Obviously, she hasn't told me anything of your sessions, but I know you're working together." He crosses his arms in front of his chest, like the gesture can help him keep his distance. "She's good. You picked well, and my texts are not snooty."

They totally are. "Whatever."

"You think I was too scared to talk to you? I fucking love you." Keegan steps forwards with an intensity in his hard gaze that's almost scary. His big hands wrap around my upper arms, holding me in place. "I love you. Of course I'm scared. And that's exactly why I'm doing this the way I am, because even if it kills me, I want you to be safe, and not stuck with someone who… well, someone like me."

He hurts. It's so obvious in his voice and his expression. It tears at my heart, because if it weren't for this whole dropping me for my own good bullshit, maybe we could've figured this whole thing out. Or if things did go to hell, at least we'd go there together.

Now we're stuck in our own private hells. Alone.

"Keegan…" I sigh. His grip on my arms is tight, but it's comforting, not painful. I meet his gaze, and it's like staring into a green sun. "I don't even know what you mean by someone like you. It's someone like you who helped me find myself. It's someone like you who gave me the strength to stand up to my mother. And as much as I hate the thought, it's someone like you who made me go see someone else when I wasn't thinking clearly enough to do it myself."

He swallows thickly, his jaw still set pugnaciously, but something softens around his eyes.

"It's someone like you I fell in love with."

He blinks, eyes shining. "Fuck," he breathes and then pulls me close so quickly I yelp.

But when he mashes his lips against mine, the urge to fight melts right away.

28

MIRANDA

He's hot to the touch, burning me up, and yet I can't get enough of him. Sliding my hands up into his hair and making tight fists, I make sure he has nowhere to go but to stay with me. The way his hands run roughly down my back until he can clutch my ass and pull me against him shows we're two of a thought.

Eventually, we have to breathe. "Miranda," he whispers.

"This doesn't change anything, just so you know," I force out between heavy breaths. "I'm still mad at you."

"I know. Should I go?" He raises his eyebrows in question, but his grip on my ass is as tight as ever.

God, I shouldn't do this.

I should push him away and make him realize that he'll never again have what he so stupidly rejected.

I should do a lot of things.

Three months ago I would've thrown myself at him without a second thought, two months ago I would've spit in his face, but today? I look him right in the eyes and search inside myself to figure out how I really feel.

Alive, for the first time since he walked away, I feel alive.

But still… "Just so you know, you're a jerk, and I hope you're going to regret pushing me away for the rest of your life."

He nods, and this time his grip slackens.

"Don't you dare let go," I hiss. If this is it, we're ending it with a bang. Maybe that way we'll be even, and I'll be stuck under his skin just like he is under mine. And if that's the way of it, then I want something good to remember him by. "Take me. Make it the best you can, because this is the last time."

He swallows and wets his lips. "Are you sure?" The muscles in his arms twitch, as if he's torn between letting go and throwing me onto the bed. "Fuck, we're just repeating our mistakes."

"Then it's a good thing I have a new therapist, isn't it? Not your problem anymore," I snap, feeling a little guilty at the flash of pain in his eyes."

"I might not be your therapist, but I still care about you, damn it."

"Oh get over yourself, Keegan. I've been through a lot worse stuff in my life than a little kinky sex." I glare him right in the eyes. "Besides, I'm stronger now, and it's not just because of Wendy. You were the push I needed to take control of my desires."

"And then I abused them," he snaps right back at me.

I shake my head. "You fell in love. Just like I did. There's nothing wrong with that, but it made things complicated. I can talk to my new therapist without wanting to tear off my clothes, which is good." I run a hand over his shoulder, wanting to memorize the feel of him. "But it's not the same.

She makes me cry sometimes, but she'll never make me scream."

He swallows hard and looks away, unable to meet my gaze. "Do you even understand how hard it was for me to stay away? I *had* to. Otherwise I would've caved the first time I saw you."

"So do it. I dare you."

"What?"

"Cave. One more time. Do me right, do me hard, do me however you want. I know what my triggers are now. If it happens again, I'll safeword, and let you take care of me. You. Not Amber, or my Mom or whoever. But you, because you're the only one who's been able to make me feel the way I do. So I dare you. Make me feel you one more time."

Maybe this is stupid, and maybe I just want some closure. Or maybe I just want to feel him in me once more before he leaves for good. And maybe, just maybe, I'm hoping that he'll realize what he'd be missing out on.

His grip tightens, and his jaw sets. Willpower and desire war in his eyes.

"I'll do anything you want me to." I lick my lips and dare to smile, just a little. Like waving steak under a dragon's nose. "Sir."

He growls, burying his face in my neck, his teeth biting at my skin while his hands drop from my ass long enough to find their way underneath my skirt before they get reacquainted. Then he physically lifts me, making me gasp in surprise as his powerful arms pull me close.

With my fingers entwined in his dark locks, I wrap my legs around him as he carries me to the back of the room. He drops me heavily on the bed, then looms over me with fiery lust in his smoldering eyes. He grips the hems of his shirt and pulls it up to reveal his muscled torso. The only moment he breaks eye contact is when the shirt goes over his head, and the intensity is already making me go gooey inside.

I raise myself up on my elbows to better watch him, licking my lips as he unbuckles his belt and pulls it loose with a crack. He tosses it on the bed next to me, like a warning. My core heats like a nuclear reactor as I imagine what he intends to do with it.

Next, he unbuttons and unzips his pants, then kicks his shoes off before pushing his jeans down over his strong thighs. When they hit the floor, he's standing there in nothing but his black boxer briefs, which are pressed out by the kind of bulge that takes a girl's breath away. As if they have a mind of their own, my knees part slowly.

"Fuck, the things you do to me," he groans, his keen eyes not having missed the slight movement. Then he hooks his thumbs in his underwear and slides them down. By bending, he covers himself, but when he stands back up, I'm treated to the most amazing view of him, all of him, and right at the center, the thick, rock hard proof of his intentions.

And then he's over me on the bed, so suddenly that I let myself fall backwards for a little distance. Instinctively, I put my hands up, pressing against his chest as if I could make him move if he really decided to give me his full weight. The fiery heat of his skin scalds my palms.

Keegan settles in, forcing my thighs apart until his thickness is pressing right against me, driving me crazy, even through my skirt and panties. With a grin, he whispers, "You're a little overdressed, aren't you?"

"You didn't really give me time."

"You had time. You were just too busy gawking."

A blush warms my face. "It's not like you weren't putting on a show."

He spreads his knees, pressing them in behind my thighs, effectively forcing my legs up in the air on either side of him. My skirt flips towards me, giving me the obscene view of his big cock pressing against my panties. "And you loved every fucking second."

No denying that.

"Here, grab your ankles." He offers me my own legs, nearly bending me over double. "I'll be right back. Don't you dare move." Then he pushes off the bed, leaving me to watch his muscles coil under his naked skin as he walks over to the lengths of black rope hanging on the wall. Picking several of them, he glances back at me over his shoulder and grins. "Good girl."

His praise warms me up inside, which I hate because I'm still mad at him, but all he has to do is give me a look and a command and I'm back to being putty in his hands. And I asked for it. Am I weak for wanting this? I want him to show me how much he's missed me, and it's a lot, from the way his hardness juts out as he comes back to the bed.

He drops the ropes next to me, where they hit the sheets with heavy thumps. With practiced efficiency, he straightens one, folding it double to make a wide cuff around my left wrist. The rest of the length he winds around my ankle, until it and my wrist are bound tightly together. A few moments later, he's done the same to the right side with his expert touch. Trussed up like this, I'm helpless to keep him from doing whatever he wants with my body.

He smirks and swats my pussy a couple of times, each whack resonating in my clit through the thin cotton. "Looking good. Let's just get you in place."

I let out a gasp as he lifts me like I weigh nothing, dropping me right in the middle of the bed. Then, quickly wrapping a new length of rope around the back of my left knee and attaching it to the headboard, he draws it tight until my foot's pointing straight up and out. Same thing on my right side. I feel like a sexy turtle, stuck on my back with my legs spread wide and nowhere to go.

A quick struggle reveals the obvious. I don't have a chance at getting free on my own. My glance flicks to my ankles, to the headboard, and then finally settles on his face. "I think you forgot to undress me first."

"Maybe."

"You're not planning on cutting my clothes off, are you?"

He gets a thoughtful expression on his face. "Would you let me?"

I consider it for a moment, because it would be kinda hot, but I just bought this skirt last week, and I'm wearing one of my good bras. "In these clothes? I'd safeword so hard before you even got close to me with the scissors. Maybe nex—" My mouth snaps shut before I can say it.

Something dark flashes over his face, and while he's smiling, the way his eyes change gives the smile a regretful quality. "Right..."

"You made your decision, okay? Let's not make this into more than it is."

He leans down and kisses my chin while his hands grab my breasts through my shirt, teasing my nipples into hard points with his thumbs. "I hate that I hurt you, but baby, we can't make it into more than it is. It's already everything."

A sharp pinch of my nipple makes me yelp in surprise. Then he nibbles at my jaw, the softness of his lips contrasting to the bite of his teeth as he works his way down my throat. I want to wrap my arms around him, grab his hair and pull him to where I want, but I'm at his mercy. I groan in frustration.

Laughing at the sound, he passes by my shirt strap and continues down my bare arm. His hands caress my sides and even through the fabric of my shirt it sends electricity arcing over my skin and raises my hairs on end.

Then he gets to the shawl still tied around my waist like a sash. "I like this. A little piratey." He laughs.

"It was cool out today."

"And you expected this to help?" He unties and holds up the silky cloth, shaking it tauntingly. "I think I can find a better use for it."

He folds it several times over itself, until it's narrow like a scarf, then drapes it over my eyes.

"What are you doing?" It's a stupid question, since I already know the answer.

"Making this a little more interesting," he murmurs in my ear as he makes sure that I can't peek. "Lift your head for me. Just for a moment." When I obey, he passes the folded shawl under my head, but ties it off to the side. "This way you won't have to lie on the knot. I might be a while."

My eyes pop open in panic behind the blindfold, not that it helps in any way. "Where are you going?"

I can sense him sliding further down the bed, then his voice comes from between my legs. "I'm not going anywhere, but I'm planning on enjoying myself. If this really is the last time—"

"Definitely," I breathe out, as much to convince myself as him.

"—then I'm going to make sure that I do this right." He places a kiss right on the outside of my panties, the pressure of his lips soft and hot through the material. I gasp in response.

"Oh… okay."

Then he kisses again, on the inside of my thigh. And again, and again, exploring my legs with his mouth and tongue. All the way up to my knees, tracing my sensitive skin. Tingles race into my core like they're trying to show him the way, but he takes his time, going maddeningly slow.

The loss of my sight makes all my other senses stronger. I listen intently for every sound. Every touch is a surprise. Even his masculine scent stands out from the smells of cleanser and well-oiled leather. He makes a game of it, moving silently and kissing, pinching or spanking me where he thinks I'll least expect it. It's making me needy, aching for him to touch me more.

"Ow!" That was a spank and it was right on my pussy. I'm more surprised than hurt, but it tingles and I cling to the sensation. Even if that's all he does, if he'll only stop teasing, I'll take it happily. "Please don't stop."

His laugh is right next to my ear. My heart beats faster. I hadn't felt him come that close. "I have no intention of stopping." He walks his fingers down my body and then the rest of him follows. Settling in between my legs, strong hands wrap around my thighs, and from that, his face has to be just about where I want him. Trapped as I am, I still try to push my hips in his direction.

He confirms his location by kissing me through my panties again, but I want—need—more than that.

"Pull them aside," I gasp. "Please. Kiss me, not my clothes."

He kisses the outside again. "Are you trying to order me around?" he asks in a soft voice that still sounds threatening, like I'm misbehaving. I can't help it. He's driving me crazy.

"N—no, I just… I can't take more of the waiting."

"Of course you can. You'll wait as long as I want you to."

"I'll use my safeword if you don't."

His immediate response is another slap, right on the pussy. I draw a sharp breath from the sting of it. "We'll have no topping from below here." He sounds almost angry. "Your safeword isn't a toy. If you use it, we will stop, and if I find out you're playing with me, then that's it, playtime's over. Is that what you want?"

"No, Sir," I reply as quickly as I can. I don't want him to stop. Not really.

"Good girl." And then he does exactly what I wanted him to, pulling my panties aside and swiping his broad tongue through my slick folds. I gasp out a moan, it feels so good to finally have him there. He does it again while his hands keep an iron grip on my thighs.

"Thank you, Sir," I get out between gasps. He's so damn good at this, and I'm already so on edge. I need him to finish me, but I know better than to start making demands. Again, I mean.

His only response is a busy tongue on my throbbing pussy. I'm good with that. Better than good. Each stroke or flick brings me just a little bit closer, my body just a little bit tighter, the burn just a little bit hotter. I flex my hips, trying to get his tongue even further inside me.

As he works his magic, I lose my power of speech. Moans and surprised breaths become my only communication each time he does something new.

At least until he suddenly gets up, leaving me a quivering needy mess with nowhere to go. "Well, I think that's good for now. I was thinking of going for a drink. Do you want anything?"

I can hear the teasing in his voice, but I'm too wound up to remember anything about proper address or staying submissive. "You get down there right this second, or I won't be responsible for my actions. I'll…" It's hard to come up with a good threat when I can't use my arms or legs. "I'll pee on you!"

"Well, not really my kink. Can we negotiate?" There's barely contained laughter in his voice.

"No! Get down there!"

"If that's what you want." He gets back on the bed, but he doesn't tongue me again. Instead he pulls the panties aside and fills me, roughly and deep, driving my breath right out of me.

That's all it takes. I was so close to the edge, and now that he's finally, finally fucking me, my whole body clenches around him as I come hard against my restraints, straining and tugging with the drive to move, but can't. I cry out in a heady blend of frustration and ecstasy. I want to wrap myself around him and claw at his back, but all I can do is take his pounding as he drives himself in and out while I come. I groan at the stimulation that refuses to stop while goosebumps cover me in tingles.

"You have no fucking idea how hard it was to hold back," he growls into my ear. "You look so amazingly fucking sexy right now, screaming and struggling and spread, just for me. I wish I could fuck you forever."

I want to tell him that he can. That it was his choice to end this and put us where we are now. God, I need to be furious with him still, but right this moment, all my energy is going to not exploding and floating away in pieces. He feels so good.

He speeds up, his hips smacking against me as he fucks me for dear life. Quiet groans slip from his throat as he approaches his finish. I can't even fuck him back, tied down like I am, but I work my Kegels, trying to squeeze his orgasm right out of him.

"Oh, fuck," he yells and then pushes deep, filling me, his come hot and wet. I keep clenching, milking him for every drop until I can't anymore. He collapses over me and kisses me frantically on the lips. "You're mine," he moans before he resumes kissing me.

I grab onto his words, pulling them inside and tucking them away in my heart before reality can crash back down. I'm not his, he saw to that, and in spite of his nice words, one frantic night at the club doesn't really change anything.

Not if he's still not willing to play for keeps.

29

KEEGAN

What the fuck just happened?

"So that's it, then?" she'd asked after I'd untied her. "I guess I'll see you around. Maybe."

I wasn't even dressed yet. When I didn't have an instant answer for her, she straightened her skirt, made sure her hair wasn't too bad of a mess, then got up and left me there. With a little bit of me still inside her and my heart bleeding from her parting stab.

I drop down heavily on the bed, still bare-ass naked and thinking about that last look she gave me over her shoulder before pushing the door open—sad, angry and still bright with afterglow, all three at once. It's a look I'm never going to forget.

She's not ready.

But what if she is? What if I'm just being an asshole who'd rather stay safe and pretend that it's all my responsibility instead of opening myself up to the risk of losing her? The Miranda who walked out that door is a totally different woman than the one who could barely meet my eyes when we first met.

How long is long enough? A month? A year?

Even if she'd forgive me for letting her go, could we really just pick up like nothing had happened? I shake my head. Of course not. This is it.

Fuck!

I wrap one of the ropes around my hand until it hurts. I can't let it end like this. I'm the Dom, right? I'm supposed to be in control, always in control. And I'm letting my insecurities run the show. Yes, I fucked up by letting our personal and professional relationships get mixed up, but does that mean we have to keep punishing ourselves forever?

Who's going to keep her safe like I can?

Goddamn it.

I fucking love her. I can't let her run away on me like this. No one has ever felt this right, so perfect. We'll figure out our future together.

But I can't do jack shit if I let her get away.

Leaping to my feet, I run for the door. I have to catch her before she gets out of here. The crowd has picked up since we slipped into the room, but I press my way through. They must see I'm on a mission, because they part quickly. Past the play area, through the corridor, and then I pop out onto the dance floor. And there she is, just about to leave on the other side of the sea of people. She's going to get out before I can stop her.

"Miranda!" It's no use. With the pounding dance music and the crowd around me, my yelling isn't close to carrying. The stairs up to the DJ booth are right here, though, so I leap the little rail and rush up to the DJ, a guy in saggy jeans and a reversed baseball cap who's waving his hand in the air while playing with one of the knobs.

His microphone is next to his mixing decks. I grab it, getting his in the progress. "Hey, what the hell are you—"

I hold my hand out to keep him at a distance while flicking the on switch. "Miranda!" I yell.

The music quiets automatically as soon as the mic goes live, which causes the single word to fill the whole club. Even though the music comes back as soon as my voice dies away, no one's dancing anymore. Everyone's staring up at me, atop the DJ booth, but my eyes are only for her.

And she turns. Confusion paints her face as she looks around.

"Up here."

Confusion gives way to shock when she spots me. She yells something, but I can't make it out over the music.

"I can't hear you, but please. Don't leave." I wet my lips. "You were right."

The DJ grins at me, obviously recognizing an idiot's plea for forgiveness when he hears one. Drawing one of the sliders on the mixer board towards him, he quiets the music to a dull roar and gives me a thumbs up. Fucking wonderful.

Self-conscious about everyone staring at me like I've just fallen from the moon, but knowing that her walking out of the building now means her walking out of my life, I continue. "I know I don't deserve you. I've acted like an ass, thinking too much of what I thought was best for you and not listening well enough to what you want. Please. Come back and we'll talk. And if I can't convince you, you're free to go and I won't bother you ever again." She yells something again, and with the music lowered, I can almost make it out. "I still can't hear you." Waving my hand, I get the DJ's attention. "Can you turn it down just a moment?"

"Sure thing, man. Good luck." He quiets the music until it's barely audible.

Miranda tries again. "Keegan, you're naked!"

What?

Fuck, I am, aren't I? That would explain some of the looks. Oh whatever, I don't give a fuck, not until I know what her answer is. "I couldn't wait. If I'd taken the time to get dressed, you would've been out the door, and I wouldn't have been able to make an ass of myself in public for you."

"And we all appreciate his ass in public, am I right?" the DJ interjects, raising a loud cheer from the dance floor.

Dammit. I'm not living this down for a while. But it's worth the risk.

Almost despite itself, a smile threatens to break out on Miranda's face. She chews her lower lip to suppress it. "Well, I guess you have to play to your strengths." The crowd, following us closely, murmurs with quiet laughter.

"So what do you say? Can we talk? I mean, somewhere a little more private, maybe?"

"Do you promise to leave your clothes off? I'm starting to like you like this." This time, her smile comes out, and it looks like hope.

The most beautiful thing I've ever seen. "Anything for you."

She nods slowly, but whether she's accepting my terms or just trying to convince herself is hard to tell. But she does come towards the DJ booth, crossing the dance floor easily as the crowd urges her on.

I hand the mic to the DJ. "Thanks. Sorry about interrupting."

"Hey man, it's cool. Not the weirdest thing to happen to me here."

Honestly, that's probably true. After a quick wave of acknowledgment, I race down the stairs and vault over the rail just in time to meet Miranda as she gets there. "Hi."

"Hi." She makes a point of looking me up and down. "I always appreciated a man in a suit."

I roll my eyes. "Come."

"Promise to talk to me like an adult who can be responsible for her own choices? Because if not, I'm right back out that door." The sternness in her voice makes it obvious that she's still angry despite her smile.

"Cross my heart. In fact, I'm going to need your help."

"Really?" She raises an eyebrow skeptically, but follows when I lead the way.

Once we're back in the private room, I sit down on the bed while Miranda elects to remain standing. She crosses her arms over her chest and watches me cautiously. "This had better be good."

I huff out a humorless laugh. "Guess being a total idiot in public only buys me so much goodwill."

She shrugs. "Any idiot can run through a BDSM club naked, commandeer the DJ booth and tell the world how dumb he's been." Her lips twitch, but the smile doesn't quite reach her eyes. "I need more than that. Why did you change your mind? Why do you need my help?"

"I honestly need your help."

"With…"

"Providing a sexy ass to spank. Willing wrists to tie. Making it impossible to get out of bed in the morning, because all I want to do is stay there and fuck you." Unbelievably enough, I'm getting hard again already, and from her glance down and little smile, she's noticed. "Listen, being a therapist means that sometimes I get too wrapped up in my own head. I was wrong when I said you didn't need me, at least partly. You don't need me as your therapist, you need me because we need each other. I want to stay with you. I want to be with you. Fuck, I don't ever want to let you go."

"You had a funny way of showing it."

"You weren't the only one that needed some space. I couldn't see past the negatives to realize that what we have together is worth the risk. My point is that I can't imagine any worthwhile life without you. I thought maybe we could try again later, much later, but the idea of being away from you, not knowing, not seeing you, not touching you… it physically hurts. Pushing you away was as much about punishing myself as protecting you. I figured that out tonight. You're the best thing to ever happen to me, and I won't let you go without a fight. Not again."

"Wow. That's… Oh God, why couldn't you just have said so to begin with?" She looks at me with big eyes, then balls her tiny fist and punches me in the shoulder, hard.

I wince, but grab her wrist and pull her in close before she can move away. "Because I'm an idiot. I forgot that we weren't just therapist and patient. We're a man and a woman who have feelings for each other. I hope, at least."

"You *are* an idiot."

"I'll have you know there are a lot of people who think I'm quite smart."

"Then they're bigger idiots." Reaching out, she puts her hand on my chest, brushing it lightly with her fingertips. Her eyes meet mine. "But you're my idiot. And if you ever, and I mean ever, try to pull anything like this on me again, I will rip your balls off, gild them and put them on my mantel. I'm not a child. If we need to talk about something, we can talk about it. I was upset when you broke things off, but if you'd sat down and talked to me, I would've agreed to find a new therapist."

"Fortunately for you, gilded balls isn't on my list of kinks, and I promise that I definitely don't think you're a child." Leaning in, I place a gentle kiss on her soft lips, loving that I'm able to taste her again. She slides a hand up into my hair, not letting me go as she responds passionately. I only intended for it to be a small gesture, but it quickly deepens into so much more.

And when her hand reaches for my eager erection, I realize that our evening has only just begun.

30

MIRANDA

I tap the door twice before I call out, "Dr. York, I'm here for my appointment."

"Excellent, Miss Larson. Come on in."

I'm wearing a white button-down blouse with a loose skirt that goes to just above my knees, while balancing on a pair of tall, black heels. My hair's wrapped up in a bun on my head. Apparently this is what Keegan's dream client looks like. I could do my own share of analyzing him for that one.

I open the door into his office—well, not his professional office, since that would be awkward, but in the spare bedroom he uses as one at home, we can fake it well enough for a little role play.

"Very good," he says.

I stand in the doorway, looking insecure, intentionally pressing my chest forwards and my ass back. The very obvious look he sends down into my cleavage might be play-acting, but the lust in his eyes definitely isn't.

"I didn't know you took clients this late, Dr. York." It's hard to keep a straight face while play acting, but I do my best. "It's so quiet here."

"Everyone else has gone home?"

"I think so, Dr. York. There's no one else around."

"Good." He taps his chin with a strong finger. "Yes, sometimes I have late sessions. Especially with clients as… fascinating as you, Miss Larson."

The dramatic pause before he says fascinating is too much. I bite my lip so I won't burst out laughing.

Somehow, he manages to keep his features completely even, but there's a mischievous twinkle in his eyes. "Are you all right?"

I nod, swallow and concentrate. "Yes, Dr. York. I'm sorry."

"Excellent. You really are an exemplary client."

I smile, and even if the compliment is just part of the fun, my cheeks heat anyway. Probably as much in anticipation as from his words. "Thank you, Sir."

"I've been reading up on your case, and apparently there's an experimental treatment that comes highly recommended. It's newly developed in Europe, so it's not well known here yet."

"That sounds… fascinating, Dr. York. Do you think it'll help me?" I ask dramatically, clasping my hands together.

It's his turn to bite his lip, but he covers it up by getting up from behind his desk and waving me over. "Face the desk, Miss Larson, and put your hands down flat on the top."

"I don't quite understand how this will help," I note, but turn around to do as he says.

"It will come clear in time. Just relax and let me do my work."

"Yes, Dr. York."

Then his hands land on my hips. "Steady now, Miss Larson."

"What are you doing?"

He softly caresses my ass through the tight skirt. "Just trust me. It's all part of the experimental treatment."

"Doctor, I don't think—"

"Shh. You don't have to." Little by little, he works my skirt up my thighs. "I'm the professional here, remember?"

I spin quickly, pushing my skirt back down. "This is hardly appropriate!" I snap, heart pumping in spite of the lighthearted atmosphere.

He grabs my hands, putting them behind my back so easily and quickly that don't have a chance to even think about resisting. When he pulls me right up against him, I'm so close I can smell him, dripping with masculinity. His voice drops to a growl. "Come now, Miss Larson. You're not going to make this difficult, are you?"

Trying to wriggle out of his grip is like trying to escape a steel trap. Keegan's so much bigger and stronger than me that it'd be scary if I didn't trust him. "Doctor, if you think I'll just let you take liberties with me—"

He laughs. "A fighter, huh? I like that. I like that very much." Keeping me easily corralled with one hand, he opens a desk drawer and pulls out a bundle of ropes.

"Doctor!"

The desk is narrow enough that when he bends me over, the edge is right at my waist on one side, and my arms and head hang off the other. A moment later, my wrists are secured to the desk's legs, and once that's done, attaching my legs the same way on the other side is a cinch. I tug at them, but I'm not going anywhere.

"Doctor!" I gasp, my helplessness real, even if the scenario isn't.

"See, now that's much better. You look beautiful trussed up like this, Miss Larson."

"What kind of treatment is this? Release me!"

His hand comes down on my ass, caressing it boldly through the skirt. "This is for your own good," he observes. "Please, Doctor. Let me go."

He pulls back and smacks my ass hard, the sound bouncing off the walls of the bedroom. I shriek in surprise.

"It would behoove you to behave, my dear Miss Larson. I hold all the cards here." He's caressing again, but he might strike again at any moment. "I would hate to have to gag such a beautiful voice as yours."

I swallow. Do I want a gag? There are other apartments in this building so someone could hear us, I guess, but I decide against it, at least for now. I'm having fun with our dialogue, even if it's like a terrible scene out of Mad Men. "I'll behave, Doctor." I submit, letting my head drop.

"Very good." He pulls my skirt up again, and this time there isn't anything I can do about it. Soon my panties are exposed, his fingers exploring me through the black silk.

I can't quite hold back a little moan when his fingers trace the outline of my folds. "Doctor, that's—"

"—exactly what you need," he finishes my sentence for me. He rubs a little harder, and despite being supposed to pretend I don't want his advances, I press my ass back at him instead, something he doesn't fail to notice. "You may think this isn't right, but your body is under no such illusion. That's why this therapy is so effective."

He comes around the desk and crouches, putting his face on level with mine. I have to crane my neck to look up at him, though, at least until he wraps his hand in my hair, undoing my bun so he can get a good grip on it. With a tug, he gets me in just the right position to kiss me firmly.

True to my role, I pinch my lips shut and try to deny him, difficult as it is. He's already got me going so hot that I want to open for him, let him run his tongue into my mouth, but I'm not supposed like this. Or at least not act like it.

Fuck it.

I kiss him back, letting my passion flow into him, catching his lip between my teeth and nipping at him. He pulls back a moment and I expect to be reprimanded for breaking character, but then he's back at me. Our tongues play, and even though the edge of the desk digs into my hips and my scalp aches from the way he's pulling it, I wouldn't stop this kiss for the world.

"I knew you'd come around." He smirks at me, and I feel like he's laughing at my inability to stay in character.

"I'm sorry, Doctor, but you kiss like a god."

His smirk goes to a full-on grin at that. "That's right. And I'm going to show you some other things I do like a god as well."

"I can't wait." Two of us can play at the smirking game.

He stands, letting go of my hair. I slump with relief, but then he's back behind me, his hard hand impacting on my ass. "Don't forget who's in control here."

"Oh, Doctor, you're so forceful," I gush.

He laughs and slaps my ass again. I'm going to feel those in the morning. There's not much protection in my panties. "You're feisty, Miss Larson. Perhaps a good spanking will put you in your place. Naughty clients get exactly what they deserve."

I can almost hear him stop breathing, as he prepares for my response.

I wait a moment, then shake my head. Nothing. After three months of ramping up our play, and working in whichever keywords we could think of that might be triggers, I seem to be rid of them. Exposure therapy, pretty much as planned, funnily enough, but we started slow and now the words don't phase me. It's so freeing.

"Pay attention, Miss Larson!" The flat of his palm impacts firmly on my ass, eliciting a grunt from me as he drives me into the table. "We don't tolerate naughty girls at my office."

I shake my head. "No, Sir. I'm sorry, Dr. York."

"That's right." He chuckles, followed by the sound of one of his drawers opening. Tied down where I am, I have no way to see what he's doing. There's rattling, as if he's pulling something out, and then two very distinct snip, snip sounds. Scissors?

"What are you—"

"You're overdressed, Miss Larson. And silly me, I seem to have made it very difficult for you to take your clothes off normally." He snips the scissors again. "But this is at least as much fun."

"Wait, you're not actually going to…" I trail off as cold steel slides along the inside of my thigh, giving me chills and raising nervous goosebumps.

"Hmm, where should I start?"

At least now I know why he insisted that I get a new outfit for tonight, but to not spend a lot of money on it. Fortunately my clothes are mostly second hand, but I didn't realize this was going to be the night he made good on his threat.

If I did, I would've worn different underwear. *Those* aren't used. "Can you—" I'm interrupted by the first cut, which goes clean through my panties and leaving nothing protecting my pussy from his touch, or whatever else he chooses to do. "Those were expensive!" I yelp.

He slaps my ass again, sending tingly sparks shooting in all directions from where he most definitely left a bright red hand print. "Bill me later." Then another snip along my right leg, and the panties fall off completely. It's not like he hasn't seen me like this before, but I feel incredibly exposed.

So what's next? My skirt? My blouse? But no, there's the clank of the scissors landing on the desk next to me, and then his mouth is between my legs and I forget all about my ruined panties. He flicks his tongue deftly between my folds, making me arch my back and grind against him in my effort to get my clit in position.

He obliges, licking like he's trying to get to the chewy center of my lollipop. I shiver and moan, squirming as surges of pure pleasure rush through me, all centered on that sensitive little button that he's swirling his tongue around.

"Oh! Kee—Dr. York! Please! I'm not that kind of girl," I cry out, not even sure if the play makes sense anymore. I'm pretty sure I showed him exactly what kind of girl I was when I pressed my pussy against his face. But I'm making an effort.

He just laughs, which sends another set of vibrations charging through me. His tongue goes wild, and then I'm past the point of putting together words, meaningful or not.

Putting his thumb to good use, he slips it inside me, forcefully thrusting it in imitation of what I'm sure is coming next while maintaining a solid grip on my ass with the rest of his hand. I fuck back at him, egging him on. "Please," I moan.

His attack intensifies, licking me harder and faster, until I start to shake, frustrated by my bonds and my inability to do anything other than receive. And then it happens, starting like a faint rumble in my ears that builds and builds until my orgasm washes over me like an avalanche, dragging me along with it.

Do I scream? I'm not even sure, but I think so. If his neighbors didn't already know that we're having sex, they definitely do now. I strain against the ropes as my whole body goes taut, a bow string aching for release, but just getting drawn further and further, until I finally collapse back on the desk, all strength gone out of me.

"See? I knew you were that kind of girl." His face is hidden, but the cocky tone in his voice is quite clear.

"Yes, Sir. You're right, Dr. York," I pant out, too exhausted to put much energy into my acting.

"At least make an effort, Miss Larson," he says sternly, adding a firm swat to my bottom for good measure.

"Yes, Doctor."

I didn't hear him pick the scissors off the table, but I definitely feel the cold of the steel sliding underneath my blouse. He works methodically, snipping from my waist and all the way up through the collar, and then down each sleeve. Then, with a couple of yanks, my bare skin presses against the hard desk, the remains of my blouse gone. It makes me feel vulnerable, even more than just being tied up does. He's not just controlling me, he's taking ownership of me down to my own clothes. Making me his, one deft cut at a time.

"You have a beautiful back," he says, sliding the blunt edge of the scissor-blade right down my spine. I shiver, feeling goosebumps chasing the trail he draws.

"Thank you, Sir."

"I don't like how this breaks up the elegant arch of it, though." He pulls my bra strap and snaps it against my back. Not very hard, but enough to sting.

No point arguing. I already know what his reply will be. "Yes, Doctor."

Two snips release the shoulder straps, and then one more next to the hooks frees it completely. I mourn the lacy bra for a moment, but I'm too turned on to let it bother me. He's promised to replace it, and as anyone who finds a sexy bra with an actual comfortable fit, I know exactly where to get more. With a quick tug, he pulls the bra out from underneath and throws it aside, leaving me in only my skirt and heels.

His hot hands come down to rest on my shoulder blades. "I think I'll leave the rest. You look delightfully sexy right now, I hope you know that."

"Thank you, Sir," I whisper, followed by a surprised, "Oh!" when something hard and fleshy bumps against my folds. I thought I was done, but my body has other plans, moving on its own to press my hips back and capture him inside me.

Keegan evades me, rotating and flexing his hips so that his hard cock rubs against me everywhere but exactly where I want it. "Don't be greedy, Miss Larson," he chides, and I really couldn't care less.

I want him in me, now!

He laughs at my desperate attempts, bumping against the insides of my thighs, rubbing across my clit and even pressing ever so lightly against my asshole. Maybe someday, but that's not what I want right now.

And then I get him. Or he lets me, but it amounts to the same thing. The tip of him is nestled between my folds and just so barely caught at my entrance. I try to push back to get him further inside, but I'm at the limits of my bondage.

"Sir, please."

"Oh, naughty, naughty. Did you really think it'd be that easy to lure me in?" He chuckles behind me, and starts to push in and out with tiny strokes, only just barely slipping inside before pulling back out. It feels nice enough, but it's in no way satisfying. I want him, and I want all of him. Then he stops, poised right at my entrance. "Tell me you're mine."

"I'm yours, Sir."

"Tell me you'll do anything I want."

"Anything, Sir. Absolutely anything you want. I belong to you."

"That's exactly what I wanted to hear," he sighs contently, then drives his hips forwards, filling me in one long stroke. I groan happily.

His weight presses me into the desk, his hips drive him deep, and tied in place I can't stop him as he uses me, fucking hard or slowly stroking exactly as he pleases. And it pleases me to be that person for him, to know that he can use me to take his pleasure. Sometimes it's enough to sweetly make love, or even be in charge every once in a while, but times like these, I love being his toy, his little plaything.

Especially because it comes with plenty of pleasure for me, too. When he made me come, it was amazing, and the feel of his thick cock plowing in and out drives me crazy, even when it's all on his terms. It takes two. I clench and press my ass up against him as well as I can as he fills me over and over.

"Miranda," he groans hoarsely into my ear. "I fucking love you." Then he drives deep one last time, his hips pressing hard against my ass while he comes, filling me with his heat. Closing my eyes tightly, I grind against him, willing him to stay where he is for as long as possible.

When he slumps over me with a low, satisfied moan, I can't help but tease. "Dr. York, I hardly think that we're on a first name basis. That would be wholly inappropriate as doctor and client."

He chuckles, and I can feel it all the way in me, my sensitive flesh tickled by the movement. "You're absolutely correct, Miss Larson. I lost my head for a moment. I beg your pardon."

God, he sounds so serious. So much for keeping my straight face any longer. I lose it in a fit of the giggles, my stomach flexing uncomfortably into the edge of the desk.

Keegan hisscs, "Jesus, when you laugh like that, it's squeezing me all over." He wraps his hands around my hips to get me to lie still, but it totally doesn't work, and then suddenly he's laughing too, and it spirals as we vibrate each other. At least until his cock, which had been softening, starts to firm up again.

"Again?" It's not a complaint.

He starts laughing again, and pulls away. "Sorry, not quite yet. Rain check?"

I pout for a moment when he slips out, but the edge of the desk is starting to get uncomfortable so he's probably right. "Yeah, that sounds good. Maybe we could do something crazy and use the bed for a change."

With a "Hah!" he sets to untying me, starting with my ankles and finally freeing my wrists. He gives me a hand so I can get back on my feet, then pulls me against him into a torrid kiss that makes me tingle all the way down to my toes.

I come up for air, legs wrapped around him and my hard nipples brushing against his chest hair. "Is it rain check time yet?"

His cock twitches against me, but Keegan just smiles and wraps his fingers in my hair. "It'll have to wait. We're supposed to meet Amber and Eric at the club in forty-five minutes."

I sigh dramatically, but I suppose he's right. "Fine. But I might just drag you off into one of the rooms, just so you know."

"I'm already looking forward to it," he says with a laugh. "I still haven't had a chance to try those candles on you."

I shiver at the thought, but I'm smiling on my way to the shower.

"Save a little water for me, okay?"

"You could come in with me, you know."

"Then we'll definitely never make it on time."

He's right, again. Frustratingly so, but I guess I can't complain too much. Cranking the water to steaming hot, I do my best to get clean, only to get dirty again later. At least if all goes as planned.

31

MIRANDA

"So you're cured?" Amber leans forward, putting her weight on her knees while staring at me with big eyes. Eric shares the black leather couch with her, but he's reclining with his arms resting on the back. Up in the club's bar area, we're sheltered from the loud music blasting over the dance floor downstairs, making it possible to talk. At least when Amber isn't constantly interjecting with questions.

"It's not like it's a disease. There are things that still make me anxious." I shrug at my excitable friend. "I'm always going to be affected by my childhood, obviously. But I've come a long way with Keegan and Doctor Wendy, and I can play now without episodes like… well, you know."

Eric, lovingly stroking his wife's back, frowns. "Yeah, that was rough. I'm glad we were there and Amber could help." He glances at Keegan, "No offense, man."

Keegan shakes his head. "None taken. I'm glad you guys were there too. Just then, I wasn't who Miranda needed."

Amber grins and takes a sip of water. "I'm so glad you two worked things out. I mean, obviously, I knew from the start that you guys would be perfect together, but it sure took you long enough to get there."

"Don't get lippy." Eric laughs while wrapping his large hand around the back of her neck and making her face him. "Lippy girls get punished." Her response is a mischievous smile, and Eric smirks before he continues, "Or just tied up and gagged somewhere so the adults can have a proper conversation."

She looks down. "That doesn't sound as much fun."

"Nope." Then he turns to me. "How's your mom doing? Amber hasn't been able to stop worrying about you two once she realized what was going on."

I hesitate, thinking back to the last time I called home. "She's doing alright. We did a session together before she left, and I managed to convince her to find someone to talk to closer to home. I don't know if she'll keep it up, but it's made things a lot easier between the two of us already.""

He nods. "She forgive Keegan yet?"

"Not really." I turn to Keegan and mouth 'sorry'. "But I think she will eventually. She's just very protective of me. Once she sees that things are good between us she'll relent."

Keegan's arm slips around me to pull me closer. I melt into what by now is the very familiar shape of him. "And then maybe you'll move in with me like I asked?"

It's tempting. "Maybe. Let's give this a little time, and then ask me again after that."

He checks the time on his phone. "That seems good. How about now?"

"Dork." I whack him on the stomach with a laugh.

"Watch it," he growls. "Eric isn't the only one here happy to punish his woman when she gets out of line."

"What's that about punishment? Can we join?" Two women approach our table with wide smiles. One's short and curvy with curly hair that seems to just do what it wants to, the other's tall and slim, with straight red hair and the brightest green eyes I've ever seen—aside from Keegan's. The shorter one's been here with Gabriel, the owner, but I don't recognize the redhead, and she'd be hard to miss.

"Dawn! Viv!" Amber gets up and gives both of them hugs. "How are you? I haven't seen you in a long time. Dawn, how's the baby?"

She smiles. "Hopefully sleeping. Not so baby anymore, though. He's starting to crawl. Nothing is safe anymore."

"Didn't bring him to the club?"

"Hah, no. But if he's awake right now, he's probably downing a bottle under his grandmother's watchful eye. Or getting whiskey-laced milk from his grandfather, but hopefully the former." She winks. "Just kidding. He should be fine," she reassures.

Gabriel and Caleb, the huge guy who was ready to separate Keegan and me when we were arguing back in the thick of things, come from the bar with two glasses each.

Dawn takes hers from Gabriel happily. "God, you have no idea how much I missed being able to drink these. But today I've pumped enough that I can have a drink without worrying about it clearing before the next time I have to nurse. Cheers!"

She takes a solid sip, while Caleb sidles up behind Viv. One hand goes around her waist after handing her a drink. She leans back against his huge frame with a content smile and a hand over her stomach.

"Sooo, Viv has something she wants to say," Dawn grins with sparkling eyes as she sits down on the couch armrest next to Eric.

"Shh," Viv responds. "We're still waiting for Paul and Em."

Amber and I look at her bemusedly, but I'm sure she's noticed the hand over Viv's belly as much as I have. I don't know these people, but it sure sounds like it might be good news.

"Holy shit, would you believe the traffic tonight?" A gruff voice comes up the stairs, followed by a solidly built man with a chiseled jaw and steely blue eyes. His right arm is around the waist of brown-haired woman. She looks strong for her size, and her baby blues are a good match for his.

"Speaking of the devil," Caleb exclaims and lets go of Viv long enough to shake hands. "Good to see you, Paul."

"Hey, man," Eric says more casually, waving from the couch. "Hey, Em."

Em waves a bit nervously. She seems like a bit of a recent arrival to the group, which makes me feel an instant kinship. "Hi everyone."

"Guess everyone's here," Caleb notes, a self-satisfied grin spreading on his face as he leans into Viv. "Should I, or do you want to do the honors?"

She rubs her tummy again and smiles. "We have an announcement to make."

"Finally getting hitched," Paul asks then shrugs to the rest of us. "Been expecting that for a while."

"Well, we're still working out the date on that, but that's not what I'm talking about."

"Oh?" Eric leans forward, and Amber's already hanging over him as if being closer will get her the announcement sooner.

"Well, there's going to be"—Viv looks around nervously, and she doesn't look like someone who gets nervous easily—"there's going to be a little Caleb. Or Viv. We decided we didn't want to know the sex until it's born."

There's a moment of silence before Amber cries out, "I knew it!" And then we all explode into congratulations and hugs. Even I get one, though we haven't even been introduced yet. Keegan solves that little issue before we resettle on the couch, him taking the far corner to make room and dragging me into his lap. Not that I mind. It's comfy and safe here.

As the new girl, caught up in a whirlwind of an announcement, I'm pretty much forgotten for a bit while the others are gushing over Viv and Caleb, but seeing their happiness makes thinking of Keegan and me inevitable. Wriggling a little, I settle more comfortably, my ass no longer getting jabbed by his hip bone, but when he moves his arm, thinking maybe I want down, I possessively wrap it back around me.

"Don't you dare let go of me," I whisper up at him.

He laughs softly into my hair. "Never."

"Do you think that'll be us one day?"

"Whoa." His tone is amused. "I was just asking you to move into my apartment, and now you're talking babies?"

"Well, not right now, obviously. But do you think we'll be happy like them?"

"I'm pretty damn happy right now."

I snuggle closer. "Mmm, me too."

"I'd be happier with you over at my place every night."

"I'll think about it," I whisper. He doesn't need to know that I already made up my mind. Let him stew in it for a little. For now, I think we're really good together, and once Mom's a little more relaxed about things I'll put in my notice with the rental office.

You obviously never know, but I have this distinct feeling that for now is quickly going to turn into forever.

And that's perfect.

THANK YOU FOR READING!

Please consider taking the time to leave a review. It really helps us independent authors a bunch!

Get news about my new releases, ARC opportunities and promotions by joining my steamy newsletter at
http://catebellerose.com/newsletter

Find my whole catalog at my website,
http://catebellerose.com/books

Or flip the page to read a preview of Make Me, the novella where the whole series began, where Gabriel and Dawn found each other.

PREVIEW: MAKE ME

A BDSM ROMANCE

Did you miss where it all started? Read on for a preview of Make Me, my first book, where you meet Gabriel and Dawn for the first time.

1

DAWN

S eriously?

Seriously?

You've got to be fucking kidding me! For the first time in forever, my lazy ass is out of bed early enough to get to work on time and then *this* happens. Goddamnit!

There are a lot of things I absolutely love about my new apartment. Central, close to work, close to nightclubs. A little noisy in the evenings, but I can sleep through most anything once I'm out. Even my alarm clock. Especially my alarm clock. There's a reason I'm already getting reprimands at the office after only a couple of months.

A thing I don't love? Street parking only, and it's tight. Moving here was a crash course in extreme parallel parking. Almost literally. Like, they should make a game show out of that, or something. Seriously. Still, after a few weeks, I kinda feel like I'm getting the hang of it.

Last night, I was really proud of how I slipped right into this spot on the first try, and it's even right outside my apartment. How awesome is that? Apparently too awesome, because I angered the parking gods, horrible beings that look down from up high, just waiting to screw over a puny little ant like me.

My car isn't much, a faded brownish-red sedan that gets me where I want to go, when I want to go there, at least most of the time. Not this time, but for once it's not my car's fault.

I check the front bumper, and the distance between it and the car in front is so short I'm not sure I can get my fingers between them. The back bumper is better, but only by like an inch or so. I can wiggle back and forth in that space all I want, but I'm still not getting out.

Fuck! I'm *this* close from pulling out my keys and going to town on those two cars. Assholes!

There's a bus, but I've never taken it. No idea what the schedule is. Not even totally sure where the stop is. It was just one of those things to check before moving here, knowing it was an option. What now? Mostly, I just want to plop my ass down and cry.

Sure, I can call work, but with my record, who's going to believe me? I can just picture Mr. Harrison now. "Young lady, you may think you can do what you want, but I *guarantee* you, that you will never become a full architect in this company if you can't even show up on time. In my day, yadda, yadda, blah, blah..." Too bad they're the only worthwhile architecture firm in town to work for.

Now I'm going to have to work overtime to make it up, and I really wanted to go out tonight. Not fair. Working late is its own kind of torture, but doesn't beat a good flogging. At least the way I see it.

Fuck.

Fuck.

"Aaarrghh!" I wanna tear something apart. Mess things up. Rip something to shreds. If I could, I'd dismantle those cars down to the last screw and spread the parts all across the city. See if those assholes park here again.

"Hey, you okay?" A deep masculine voice sends heat racing straight down to my core.

I turn, and immediately wish his first impression wasn't of me screaming at my car like a lunatic. The most handsome man I've seen all day, maybe my whole life, arches his eyebrow and looks at me.

He's tall. I'm short, so everyone looks tall, but he's taller than that. Makes-me-feel-like-a-little-girl tall. His leather jacket's open over a black t-shirt that's stretched tight across his broad chest. Not bulging, but hard. Strong. And those arms. Bet he could give a good spanking to a girl in need.

I swallow and crane my neck, my gaze exploring all the way up, past his powerful shoulders and strong neck, over a chiseled jaw and a pair of full smirking lips that look made for kissing. Bright under short and spiky black hair, a hungry set of deep hazel eyes, flecked with green and brown, are crinkled in amusement.

"Uh, hi." That's right, Dawn. Dazzle him with your smart reply and draw him in with your witty repartee. Fuck, I'm screwed.

"Hi yourself." That voice could melt ice, it's so hot. Deep and with just a little hint of scratch. I bet he's a growler. I like that, when they're gruff.

"So... I was passing by and couldn't help over-hearing your expression of... frustration?" His eyes lock to mine, and I know I can never tell that man a lie to his face. I'd break down. God, those are amazing eyes.

I realize he's waiting for an answer. Right. Stop mooning, Dawn. "I, uh... well, my car's stuck."

"Stuck?"

"Yeah, like parked in. Look at this bullshit."

His smirk turns to a crooked grin, like he didn't expect me to swear, or something.

Yep, that's me. A delicate flower. If he only knew, but he doesn't, and it's not something I'll blurt out to someone I just met, so I just wave at the car.

"Those fuckers made a sandwich out of my car, and now I can't get to work." The frustration's back and the rest just pours out of me. "And now I'll get reprimanded again, and if Mr. Harrison's not feeling forgiving, I'll lose my apprenticeship, and get my ass kicked out on the street and be without a fucking job, and it's all because I can never get the fuck out of bed on time, and be respectful and not fuck up everything like I always do, and…"

He cuts me off with a finger to my lips. "Shhhh."

A bit close for comfort, but it's hard to get angry at a smile like that. Besides, he's right. "Sorry, I know you don't want to hear it. Why would you care, right? Didn't mean to dump on you. Just frustrated, y'know?"

"Sounds like you've got a lot on your plate. If you had time, I'd stick around and listen to every single word." Obviously he sees me screw my face up in disbelief. "Listen, I don't think I can fix everything for you, but I can fix this. Gimme your keys."

"What?"

"Your car keys. Give them to me."

I glance at my car, then back at him. Is he like a parking ninja or something? He's pretty ripped, but I don't think he can lift my car out. Wouldn't need my keys for that anyway. He could just take them and run away, but there's something about him. I trust him, though I don't know why. Maybe because he's willing to listen. Reaching into my pocket, I dig them up and hold them out to him.

His grin widens as he takes them. He talks as he rounds the car behind mine so he can get to the driver's seat. "I get the whole getting up late thing, by the way. I'm actually on my way home from work. Maybe you just need a job that lets you stay up late and sleep late. Worked for me."

"If you know of any late night architect firms, let me know."

He stops with his hand on the roof of the car, and laughs, a bark deep in his chest. "Guess that's a tough one. Architect, huh? Cool."

The keys jingle as he finds the lock and shoves them in. The door creaks when he opens it, like it always does. "You could oil this, you know."

He looks unsure for a moment, which doesn't suit him. Then he reaches in, finds the handle for moving the seat and pushes it back as far as it can go. Even then, he's way too big for my car. It's like they built the car the wrong size. Still, he gets the key in and starts it up. Where does he think he's gonna go? I watch with deep interest.

Just as his hand shifts into reverse, I realize what he's about to do. Seriously? He throws his thick arm over the back of the passenger seat, looks over his shoulder and pushes the gas. Gently. The car doesn't jump backwards or anything, but I cringe when my back bumper touches the asshole bumper. Is this even legal?

My car stops, blocked by the other car. Maybe he just knows some clever wiggle technique. Nah. The engine revs and the front dips a little as he steps down. My car sounds angry, frustrated, a lot like me. No way this'll work. That guy's hot as anything, but he's gotta be nuts.

Then something happens. The cars move, a creaky sound like a whiny protest coming from the asshole car. He pushes harder, and the whiny protest grows into a panicked squeal. My hands go to my ears while I watch gleefully. That couldn't possibly be doing good things to that car's gearbox.

Inch by inch, the cars move until they've gone almost a foot. Is that enough? My guardian angel lets up on the gas, shifts and drives forward until my front bumper kisses the back bumper of the other car. Again?

More revving, more pressure, more squealing, and that car moves too. This guy's over the top. Who does that? He does, I guess. There's a sharp crack, and suddenly the cars move easily. Fuck, was that the hand break? Will I be responsible for this? I don't know much about cars, but sharp cracks when forcing a car to move sound really expensive.

On the bright side, my car's free, and looks unharmed. Maybe a couple of scratches on the bumpers, but who looks at those anyway? Just plastic.

He shuts off my car and climbs out. "You probably have to adjust your seat, but I think you're good to go."

"You're fucking crazy, you know that?" I'm grinning so hard it almost hurts. "Thank you. You've saved my ass something fierce."

His answering grin makes my stomach knot. Never mind forcing cars to move, can a face that handsome be legal? "It's a nice ass. It deserves some saving."

"What? I…"

"Shouldn't you be getting to work? You said something about getting fired."

"Oh shit. Yeah."

He tosses the keys to me, which, amazingly enough, I catch. Go me. When I look up, he's already walking away, like his work here's done.

"Hey, wait."

He turns.

"Can I thank you for this some way? I mean, later? Like buy you a coffee or something? What's your name?"

That smile again. "Gabriel." He waves. "See you around." He walks off.

"I'm Dawn!" I yell it at his back.

"Nice to meet you, Dawn." I want to swoon. Is swooning out of fashion these days? I watch him until he turns a corner and disappears.

Shit, I need to hurry, not stand here and moon. Seat, mirror, keys in the ignition. The car turns over and I get the hell out. I'm late, but not *that* late, and I can make it up if I hurry. At least traffic's light. If I get there early enough, I'll still have time to visit the club.

Gabriel. I laugh. He really is my guardian angel. I had no idea angels were batshit insane, though.

2

DAWN

You wouldn't think it was possible to make a flogging boring. Seriously. Same speed, same rhythm, same strength. He wants me to count, but I stopped to get a rise out of him. He hasn't even mentioned it. Just the same limp-wristed stroke over and over.

The sawhorse is biting into my hip, too. Not sure if it's uncomfortable, or I can pretend that it's part of the play. Wish I was taller. At least my feet would touch the ground then.

My nose itches, but my hands are bound, stretched out along the sawhorse on either side of me. Kinda stuck staring at the floor while um… Dennis? While Mr. Uninspired works the exact same spot on my ass, and if my hands were free, works would be in air quotes.

I should say something, but I'd probably crush his fragile ego. For playing at domination, he doesn't exactly flog with confidence. Not my most amazing BDSM experience, to put it mildly, and there haven't even been that many.

The club's packed, but none are watching us. Bet we bore them too, even with our prime spot near the center of the floor. I'm still wearing my bra and panties, so they don't even have my naughty bits to gawk at.

Other players are having more fun. Can't see them through the crowd since I'm kinda tied up here, but I hear them. Moans, screams. Yelps of pain. Someone's coming, or she's really good at faking it. I'm envious.

I see shoes. I've seen a lot of shoes today, but these stopped right in front of me. Nice. Leather. Men's. I crane my neck, trying to look up the denim-covered legs, but I can't see very far from this position. Nice legs, though.

He crouches and pair of newly familiar green and brown speckled hazel eyes sparkle at me with amusement. What the hell is Gabriel doing here? Did he follow me? Oh fuck, I've got a stalker. Pretty damn good-looking for a stalker, though, I'll give him that. Already he's making my heart beat faster than Dennis is.

He doesn't say anything. Doesn't want to interrupt the scene, I guess, but he raises his eyebrows questioningly at me. I grimace, trying to communicate how bored I am. Save me.

I think he gets it, but he drops one eyebrow and leaves the other one up, suddenly skeptical rather than curious. Or is that judgemental? Just a twitch? I dunno. As amazingly expressive as faces are supposed to be, a few good words go a long way.

With a quick wink, he stands. Great, he's bored too. Or did he have another plan? Anything to save me from the doldrums.

"Hi." It's Gabriel's voice, but he's not talking to me. "Um, Dennis, is it? Sorry to interrupt your scene. You look like you're having a great time, and that's what this club's all about."

"Uh... right?"

Ah, Dennis, you domming alpha, you.

"Listen, I'm not here to criticize or anything, but I couldn't help notice your pet."

"Yeah?" Pride creeps into Dennis's voice, like he owns me or something. "She's pretty fucking hot, huh?"

"That she is, my friend. Fucking gorgeous. But you know what? She owes you an apology."

What?

"What?" Dennis is as confused as me.

"Well, she's just hanging there, looking bored and that makes you look bad. If she's not having a good time, then it's her responsibility to let you know."

Oh God. That fucker! I thought we shared a little moment there, but all he does is humiliate me. Oh, he's gonna hear it. "Gabri…"

"Shut up, Pet." There's steel in Gabriel's voice. Hard, lethal steel. Hard, lethal, goddamn sexy steel. "Don't speak until spoken to. You're already in enough trouble."

I feel bad. Not for being bored, but because those few words already have me more turned on than the last fifteen, twenty minutes of flogging have.

"She did stop counting, but I thought it was subspace or something, you know? Really, she's bored?"

Oh God, he's not gonna cry, is he? He sounds heartbroken.

Dennis sighs. "Is this true, Dawn?"

As soon as I'm free, I'm going to kick Gabriel's ass. I sigh. "Yes."

"Alright. Fine. I'll untie you. Maybe it's just not our thing, I guess."

"Hold it." Gabriel's voice cuts through like a meat cleaver. "I didn't say let her go. She owes you an apology. She's humiliated you, man."

"No, it's alright, I'll just…"

"It's not alright. Listen, if you're not going to punish her, give her to me. I'll handle it. It's her responsibility as your sub to let you know things aren't working for her."

Now that's interesting. Very interesting. I swallow, wondering what Gabriel has in mind. Something tells me it's going to be in a different league.

"I suppose you could…"

"Great, come around here a sec." Two pairs of shoes appear, stopping in front of me. Gabriel crouches. "Pet, apologize to your Dom."

It's a gamble, but I can't help it. Craning my neck so I can see him, I put as much sneer into my answer as I can. "No."

He grins, but doesn't say anything. "One more chance, Pet."

"No." No more, no less.

Gabriel stands and steps behind me. "Dennis, what are your safewords?"

"Um, right… we don't…"

I can almost hear Gabriel's eyes rolling in his head as he sighs. "Fine. Yellow, I'm going too hard or something's wrong. We talk and work it out. Red, I'm way outta hand and we stop. Doesn't have to be forever, but something major must change before we continue. Got it?"

A pregnant pause.

"Pet? Do you get it."

Oh, he was talking to me. Of course. "Yes."

"Good. Now, are you going to apologize?"

"No."

"Suit yourself."

A swish and a thwack. Fiery streaks of red hot pain slash across my ass, and I scream. Fucking hell, he doesn't mess around.

"Apologize."

I chew my lower lip, considering. My ass burns, but my pussy's suddenly gushing. He gets me, what I crave, what I need. There's only one right answer. "No."

Thwack!

Oh, Jesus H. Christ on a stick. My thighs this time, right where they meet my ass, some of the tendrils criss-crossing the first ones. I can only imagine the bright red welts. But God, I don't want him to stop. "No."

"You're only making this harder on yourself."

Thwack! Thwack!

My upper back, first one side, then the other. Hard, solid hits, driving pain deep into my chest cavity. I have to catch my breath, hearing it ragged in my throat. I whimper. He's making me fucking whimper.

My reply comes out like a croak. "No."

I brace, but nothing happens. Opening my eyes, I see Dennis is still there, his shoes shifting back and forth uncomfortably. He can't even handle someone else doing the job properly. Who ever let him put a flogger in his hand to begin with? Gabriel's shoes appear.

"Listen, Dennis."

"Y… yeah?"

"I think this might take a while. Why don't you head to the bar. Drinks are on me tonight. Just let Mike know Gabe sent you. If she comes around, I'll bring her over to apologize. Sound good?"

"Uh… yeah. Thanks."

"Hey, no worries. Listen, ask Mike if Miss Victoria's around. I think she might be right up your alley. You know her?"

"No, don't think I…"

"You'll like her. Off you go. I'll take care of our little brat here."

"Right. Thanks." He's off like his ass is on fire.

I dare a question. "Who's Miss Victoria?"

Gabriel's back down to my level, a boyish grin splitting his face. "Best Domme in town. That guy's as much a Dom as I'm a sub. I think they'll get along great."

I can't hold back the giggle.

He's at my throat immediately, his huge hand wrapping around so far his fingers almost touch. I want to swallow, but I can't against the pressure. "Laughing at your former master? I'm not done with you, you know. You still owe that guy an apology."

Being defiant isn't easy when you can hardly breathe. "What, you're gonna make me?" It comes out as a wheeze.

"Fuck yeah. Unless you safeword."

I only think for a second. "No."

He lets go, and I draw a deep breath. Air. Sweet, sweet air.

"Well, back to it, then." His voice is a growl that makes me shudder and my stomach drop. Even the soft material of my bra feels rough on my tight nipples, and my thighs feel sticky. This is what I want.

Smack!

Ow! That was his hand! Right onto my left asscheek and staying there, gripping the flesh hard in his rough fingers. It hurts and feels so good, so fucking good.

"You know, I can do this all night. I've got nowhere else to be, but I'll have to get someone to drive you home, cause you sure as hell won't be walking. Or you can apologize to the man." Husky, his voice cuts into me.

I quiver, realizing he can do anything he wants to me and I'll let him. "I won't."

Smack!

The same spot again, pain on pain, compounding. I sob, my shoulders shaking.

"You will, if it takes me all night."

His hand adds heat to my already burning ass, over and over. I scream. A crowd has gathered around us, watching him work his magic, watching me squirm beneath him. Every strike shakes my flesh and pushes me against the sawhorse. My feet kick uselessly. My ass hurts, tendrils of pain snaking their way all the way out to my toes and fingertips.

I'm crying, salty tears sliding down my cheeks, dropping to the floor. I'm reaching my limit, but I don't want to give up, don't want to give him the satisfaction. He's stern, but I'm tougher. At least, that's what I want to think, but fuck, it hurts.

He's stopped. All I feel is burning, stinging pain, but he's not spanking me anymore. Are we done? Did I win? I want to gloat, but at the same time I'm disappointed. It couldn't be that easy, could it? I wince and twitch. Not *that* easy, I suppose.

Smack!

It's the hardest one yet, driving into my ass, pain exploding like a firecracker. It's the last straw, and I gasp, sob and whimper all at once, my head hanging in defeat.

Shoes. He crouches in front of me. Wiping the tears off my face with his thumb, he studies me. "Look at me."

I twist my head to meet his eyes, his glinting, green-flecked hazel eyes that seem to stare right into the deepest parts of me. They crinkle in amusement, making crow's feet. "All it takes is an apology. Nothing more, and we can end this. We'll find him, you'll kneel like a good girl and tell him you're sorry for ruining his scene. That's it."

I don't want to lose, but I want him to win. What do I do? I'm exhausted. I won't be able to sit for a week. He's read me so well, taking me right to my limit. I do the only thing I can do. I surrender.

"I'll…" The crying's made my nose run, and I pull it back in with an indelicate sound. "I'll apologize."

Immediately, he's untying me, releasing my sore wrists and lowering me carefully from the sawhorse. I collapse right into his arms, and he holds me, comforting me, his large arms enveloping me as he pulls me close. I close my eyes, resting my head against his chest.

"You're a tough master." I mumble it into his shirt.

"You're a tough customer, babe." There's a grin in his voice, but I just nestle in closer, not caring. His hands stroke my arms while I recover.

WANT TO READ MORE?

Get Make Me: A BDSM Romance at Amazon
today!

ABOUT THE AUTHOR

There's something magical about the games of dominance and submission. The excitement of giving total control to the one you love, knowing that he will take you places you never thought you could go. The absolute trust in a man who loves you, who wants to challenge you, who wants to bring out the best in you.

It's love and total devotion in its purest sense, and that's what I love to write about, at least when I'm not wrangling kids and taking care of my family!

catebellerose.com
cate@catebellerose.com
facebook.com/cate.bellerose

Printed in Great Britain
by Amazon

69296933R00241